His mouth found hers again, and this time the kiss was hot enough to brand cattle.

A fiery mix of passion and lust, making her forget she didn't kiss strangers like this, on an open dance floor with half the town watching. But Brooks didn't let up and she couldn't pull back or move away, it was that good.

She played with the curling ends of his hair.

He slid his hands lower on her back.

She tucked herself into him.

He groaned and kissed her harder.

The music ended and they hardly noticed. She stared into his blue eyes.

"What now?" he rasped. "You want another dance?"

She shook her head. "I need air."

He took her hand and led her off the dance floor and out the door of the C'mon Inn. They went around back to an iron and wood bench near a walled garden. "Would you like to sit?" he asked, and before she could answer, he took a seat and reached for her, giving her the option of where on the bench she wanted to plop down.

She chose his lap.

*

The Texan's One-Ni[...]
the Dynasties: The New[...]
chaos consume a Chic[...]

Dear Reader,

I can't imagine having to search for a long-lost anyone, but real estate mogul and Chicagoan Brooks Newport finally ends his months-long search for his biological father, Beau Preston, in Cool Springs, Texas—aka Small Town, USA. For Brooks it was a labor-intensive, painstaking road to locate his dad after the true circumstances of their separation finally became clear to both father and son.

But for Brooks, their reunion comes with a surprise wrinkle along the way. Ruby Lopez, the Latina spitfire he'd met at the C'mon Inn the night before, is just as happy tossing a man over her petite shoulders as she is training thoroughbreds. Soon, Ruby becomes a temptation, and as off-limits as one woman can get when Brooks discovers her strong ties to the Preston family. Might I add, the raven-haired beauty keeps the wannabe cowboy on the tips of his Justin-booted toes and throws poor Brooks completely off-kilter.

But does she flip him on his backside? You'll just have to read on to see.

I'm a horse lover by nature, and so researching training techniques and describing the beautifully groomed and modern but rustic Look Away Ranch was a joy for me. Twinkling lights strung across the perimeter, holly wreaths and poinsettias make for a postcard Christmas at Look Away. What could be better than a cowboy in the making, wild stallions, strategically placed mistletoe, surprise presents under the tree and finding true love where you least expect it?

The Texan's One-Night Standoff is my gift to you.

Happy holidays and happy reading!

Charlene

CHARLENE SANDS

———

THE TEXAN'S ONE-NIGHT STANDOFF

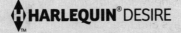

Special thanks and acknowledgment are given
to Charlene Sands for her contribution to the
Dynasties: The Newports miniseries.

Recycling programs
for this product may
not exist in your area.

ISBN-13: 978-0-373-73499-3

The Texan's One-Night Standoff

Copyright © 2016 by Harlequin Books S.A.

Printed in U.S.A.

www.Harlequin.com

Charlene Sands is a *USA TODAY* bestselling author of more than forty romance novels. She writes sensual contemporary romances and stories of the Old West. When not writing, Charlene enjoys sunny Pacific beaches, great coffee, reading books from her favorite authors and spending time with her family. You can find her on Facebook and Twitter, write her at PO Box 4883, West Hills, CA 91308, or sign up for her newsletter for fun blogs and ongoing contests at charlenesands.com.

Visit her Author Profile page at Harlequin.com, or charlenesands.com, for more titles.

To my very talented editor, Charles Griemsman,
who is also a wonderful person and someone
I call friend. Thanks, Charles, for all you do!

One

Brooks Newport swiveled around on the bar stool at the C'mon Inn, his gaze fastening on the raven-haired Latina beauty bending over a pool table, challenging her opponent with a fiercely competitive glint in her eyes. With blue jeans hugging her hips and a cropped red plaid blouse exposing her olive skin, the lady made his mouth go dry. He wasn't alone. Every Stetson-wearing Texan in the joint seemed to be watching her, too.

His hand fisting around the bottle, Brooks took a sip of beer, gulping down hard. The woman's moves around the pool table were as smooth and as polished as his new Justin boots.

"Five ball, corner pocket," she said, her voice sultry with a side of sass, as if she knew she wasn't going to miss. Then she took her shot. The cue ball met its mark and sure enough, the five ball rolled right into the pocket.

She straightened to full height, her chest expanding to near button-popping proportions. She couldn't have been more than five-foot-two, but what she had in that small package was enough to make him break out in a sweat. And that was saying something, since he'd come to Texas for one reason, and one reason only.

To meet his biological father for the first time in his life.

He'd spent the better part of his adulthood trying to find the man who'd abandoned him and his twin brother, Graham in Chicago. Sutton Winchester, his bitter older rival and the man Brooks thought might be his biological father turned out not to be his blood kin after all. Thank God. But Sutton had known the truth of his parenthood all along, and the ailing man, plagued by a bout of conscience—or so Brooks figured—had finally given up the information that led to the name and location of his and Graham's father.

Brooks would have been speaking with his real father at Look Away Ranch in Cool Springs right now if he hadn't gotten a bad case of nerves. So much was riding on this. The trek to get to this place in time, to solving the mystery surrounding the birth of the Newport twins, as well as his younger brother Carson, would finally come to fruition.

So, yeah, the powerful CEO of the Newport Corporation from Chicago had turned chicken. Those bawking noises played out in his head. He'd never run scared before and yet, as he was breezing through this dusty town, the Welcome sign and Christmas lights outside the doors of the C'mon Inn had called to him. He'd pulled to a stop and entered the lodge, in need of a fortifying drink and a good night's rest. He had a lot to think about, and meeting Beau Preston in the light of day seemed a better idea.

He kept his gaze trained on the prettiest thing in the joint. The woman. She wielded the pool cue like a weapon and began wiggling her perfectly trim ass in an effort to make a clean shot. He sipped beer to cool his jets, yet he couldn't tear his gaze away. He had visions of bending over the pool table with her and bringing them both to heaven.

Long strands of her hair hung down to touch her breasts, and as she leaned over even further to line up her shot, those strands caressed green felt. She announced her next shot and *bam*, the ball banked off the left side and then ricocheted straight into the center pocket.

The whiskered man she was playing against hung his head. "Man, Ruby. You don't give a guy a chance."

She chuckled. "That's the rule I live by, Stan. You know that."

"But you could miss once in a while. Make it interesting."

So her name was Ruby. Brooks liked the sound of it, all right. It fit.

He had no business lusting after her. Woman trouble was the last thing he needed. Yet his brain wasn't doing a good job of convincing his groin to back off.

The game continued until she handed the older guy his vitals on a silver platter. "Sorry, Stan."

"You'd think after all these years a man could do better against a teeny tiny woman."

She grinned, showing off a smile that lit the place on fire, then set a sympathetic hand on the man's shoulder and reached up to kiss his cheek.

The old guy's face turned beet red. "You know that's the only reason I endure this torture. For that kiss at the end."

Her deep, provocative chuckle rumbled in Brooks's ears. "You're sweet for saying that, Stan. Now, go on home to Betsy. And kiss your sweet grandson for me."

Nodding, Stan smiled at her. "Will do. You be good now, you hear?"

"I can always try," she said, hooking her cue stick on the wall next to a holly wreath.

Stan walked off, and Ruby did this little number with her head that landed all of her thick, silky hair on one shoulder. Brooks's groin tightened some more. If *she* was any indication of what Cool Springs was like, he was quickly gaining an affinity for the place.

The woman spotted him. Her deep-set eyes, the color of dark cocoa, met his for a second, and time seemed to stop. Blood rushed through his veins. She blinked a time or two and then let him go, as if she recognized him to be an out-of-towner.

He finished off his beer and rose, tossing some bills onto the bar and giving the barkeep a nod.

"Hey, sweet doll," a man called out, coming from the darkest depths of the bar to stand in front of her. "How about giving me a go-round?"

Ruby tilted her head up. "No thanks. I'm through for the night."

"You ain't through until you've seen me wield my stick. It's impressive." The big oaf wiggled his brows and crowded her against the pool table.

She rolled her eyes. "Pleeeze."

"Yeah, babe, that's exactly what you'll be crying out once we're done *playing*."

"Sorry, but if that's your best come-on line, you're in sad shape, buster."

She inched her body away, brushing by him, trying not to make contact with the bruiser. But the jerk grabbed her arm from behind and gave a sharp tug. She struggled to wiggle free. "Let go," she said.

Brooks scanned the room. All eyes were still on Ruby, but no one was making a move. Instead they all had smug looks on their faces. Forget what he'd thought about this town; they were all jerks.

The muscles in his arms bunched and his hands tightened into fists as Brooks stepped toward the two of them. He couldn't stand by and watch this scene play out, not when the petite pool shark was in trouble. "Get your hands—"

The words weren't out of his mouth before Ruby elbowed the guy in the gut. "Oof." He doubled over, clutching his stomach, and cursed her up and down using filthy names.

Crap. Now she was in deep. The guy's head came up; the unabashed fury in his eyes was aimed her way. Brooks immediately pulled his arm back, fists at the ready, but before he could land a punch, Ruby grabbed the guy's forearm. The twist of her body came so fast, Brooks blinked, and before he knew it, she'd tossed the big oaf over her shoulder WWF-style and had him down for the count. As in, she'd laid him out flat on his back.

Someone from the bar groused, "No one messes with Ruby unless she wants to be messed with."

Apparently the oaf hadn't known that. And neither had Brooks. But hell, the rest of them had known.

She stepped over the man to face Brooks, her gaze on the right hook he'd been ready to land. "Thanks anyway," she said, out of breath. Apparently she wasn't Supergirl. The effort had taxed her, and he found himself enjoying how the ebb and flow of her labored breaths stretched the material of her blouse.

He stood there somewhat in awe, a grin spreading his mouth wide. "You didn't let me do my gladiator routine."

"Sorry. Maybe next time." Her lips quirked up.

Behind her, the bartender and another man began dragging the patron away.

"Does that happen often?" he asked her.

"Often enough," she said. "But not with guys who know me."

He rubbed at his chin. "No. I wouldn't imagine."

He kept his gaze trained on her, astonished at what he'd just witnessed. Her eyes danced in amusement, probably at his befuddled expression. And then someone turned up the volume on the country song playing, and his thoughts ran wild. He was too intrigued to let the night end. This woman wasn't your typical Texas beauty queen. She had spunk and grit and so much more. Hell, he hadn't been this turned on in a long, long time.

A country Christmas ballad piped in through the speakers surrounding the room. "Would you like to dance?" he asked.

She smiled sweetly, the kind of smile that suggested softness. And he would've believed that if he hadn't seen her just deck a man. A big man.

Her head tilted to the left, and she gauged him thoughtfully.

He was still standing, so that was a plus. She didn't find him out of line.

"Sure. I'd like that, Galahad."

"It's Brooks."

"Ruby."

She led him to the dance floor and he took over from

there, placing his hand on the small of her back, enfolding her other hand in his. Small and delicate to big and rough. But it worked. *And how*, did it work.

He began to move, holding her at arm's length, breathing her in as they glided across the dance floor.

"I thought you were in trouble back there," he said.

"I gathered."

"Are you a black belt or something?"

"Nope, just grew up around men and learned early on how to take care of myself. What about you? Do you have a knight in shining armor complex or something?"

He laughed. "Where I come from, a man doesn't stand by and watch someone abuse a lady."

"Oh, I see."

"Apparently I was the only other guy in the place who didn't know you could handle yourself."

She was looking at him now, piercing him with those cocoa eyes and giving him that megawatt smile. "It was sorta sweet, you coming to my rescue." Was she flirting? *Man, oh man.* If she was, he wasn't going to stop her.

"I was watching you, like every other guy at the bar."

"I like to play pool. I'm good at it," she said, shrugging a shoulder. "It's a great way to blow off steam."

"That's exactly why I stopped into the bar myself. I needed to do the same."

"You get brownie points for not saying the obvious."

"Which is?"

Her lips twitched and she hesitated for a second, as

if trying to decide whether to tell him or not. "That you know a better way to blow off steam."

Her raven brows rose, and he stopped dancing for a second to study her. "You must drive men wild with your mouth."

She shook her head, grinning. "You're sinking, Brooks. Going under fast."

"I was talking about your sass."

She knew. She was messing with him. "Most men hate it."

"Not me. It's refreshing."

He brought her closer, so that the tips of her breasts grazed his shirt and the scent of her hair tickled his nostrils. She didn't flip him over her shoulder with that move. She cuddled up closer. "So far, I have two brownie points," he said. "What can I do to earn another?"

Her gaze drifted to his mouth with pinpoint accuracy. Air left his chest. A deep hunger, like none he'd experienced before, gnawed into his belly.

"You'll think of something, Galahad."

The stranger's lips touched hers, a brief exploration that warmed up her insides and made her question everything she'd done since setting eyes on this guy. Usually she wasn't this brazen with men. She didn't flirt and plant ideas in their heads. But there was something about Brooks that called to her. He had manners. And he knew how to speak to a woman. He seemed familiar and safe in a way, even though they'd never met before. He wasn't hard on the eyes either, with all that blond hair, thick and wavy and catching the collar of his zillion-dollar shirt. He was as citified as they came, even if he wore slick boots and sported five-o'clock stubble. As soon as she'd spotted him at the bar, she knew he didn't belong. Not here, in a dusty small town out in the middle of nowhere. Cool Springs wasn't exactly a mecca of high society, and this guy was that and then some. His coming to her rescue, all granite muscles and fists ready to pummel, was about the nicest thing a man had done for her in a long while.

Trace came to mind, and she immediately washed his image from her head. She wasn't going to think about her breakup with him. He was six months long gone, and she'd wasted enough time on him.

Instead she wrapped her arms around Brooks's neck and clung to him, her body sizzling from the heat surrounding them. He began to move again, slower, closer, his scent something expensive and tasteful. Her nerves were raw. Something was happening to her. Something unexpected and thrilling. Her life was too predictable lately, and it was time to change that.

His mouth found hers again, and this time the kiss was hot enough to brand cattle. A fiery mix of passion and lust, making her forget she didn't kiss strangers like this, on an open dance floor with half the town watching. But Brooks didn't let up, and she couldn't pull back or move away. It was that good.

She played with the curling ends of his hair.

He slid his hands lower on her back.

She tucked herself into him.

He groaned and kissed her harder.

The music ended and she hardly noticed.

She stared into his blue eyes.

He gave her a smile.

Her body was shaking.

He was trembling, too.

"What now?" he rasped. "You want another dance?"

She shook her head. "I need air."

He took her hand and led her off the dance floor and out the door of the C'mon Inn. Clouds shadowed half the full moon, and the bite of December air should've cooled her down. But Brooks kept her close to his side, his body shielding her from the cold. Any shivering she was doing was caused by the man beside her and not the dropping winter temperature. He led her around back, where a bench made of iron and wood sat unoccupied near a walled garden. "Would you like to sit?" he asked, and before she could answer, he took a seat and reached for her, giving her the option of where on the bench she wanted to plop down. She chose his lap.

His satisfied smile was her reward, and she wrapped her arms around his neck. "You're beautiful, Ruby. You probably hear that all the time." His hand grazed her neck as he held her hair back to nibble on her throat. Then his tongue moistened her skin as he laid out a row of sensual kisses there. Her insides went a little squishy from his tender assault. Whatever this was, it was happening fast. His rock-hard erection pressing against her legs told her he was as turned on as she was.

"Not really. I tend to scare men off." By her own choosing, she warded off men's advances before giving them half a chance. She'd been waiting around for Trace, hoping he'd come back to her, but that hadn't happened. And now she found pleasure in this man's arms. She didn't know a thing about him, other than her instincts said he was a decent man.

"Little ole you," he whispered softly before claiming her lips again. The taste of alcohol combined with his confidence was a sweet elixir to her recent loneliness. His mouth pressed hers harder, and the tingles under her skin bumped up another notch. "You didn't scare me off."

"Maybe that's why I'm here with you."

"I like the sound of that." The rasp in his voice intensified.

They stopped talking long enough to work up a sweat. Sharp and quick tingles ran up and down her body, and her breaths came in short bursts. She was aware of him at every turn. His well-placed touches made her tremble. His kisses swamped her in heat. Brooks wasn't far behind. His passion swept her up, and the proof of his desire strained the material of his dark pants. She arched her body in a curving bow, craving more, wanting his hands on her everywhere. Under her cropped shirt, her nipples tightened, and an ache throbbed below her waist.

Finally Brooks touched her breasts, and the beauty of the sensation purred from her lips. "Oh, yes."

Low guttural sounds surfaced from his chest, groans of pleasure and want as his hands moved over her body, palms wide, so he could grasp every inch of her. He flattened her erect nipples, followed the curve of her torso and dipped down lower to her hips. He ran his hands along her legs, up and down her thighs, and from under her jeans she felt the burn on her skin.

Laughter coming from patrons leaving the inn rang in her ears.

Brooks stopped and listened.

The sounds became softer and eventually ceased. Thank goodness those people weren't coming back here.

"Ruby, honey. I'm not one for public groping." He hesitated a second. "I have a room."

She bit down on her lower lip, his taste lingering on her mouth. It helped her make the decision. She wasn't ready for this to end. "Take me there."

Ruby drove him wild and crazy with want. Yeah, he'd been without a woman for several months, but this woman was more than he'd ever dreamed of. This woman, he couldn't have even imagined. She was the hottest female he'd met in his life, and she was exactly what he needed to...ah, hell, *blow off steam*. Her flipping that oaf on his back had been just the beginning. From then on, every word that came out of her mouth, every tempting gesture and coy smile, had been perfect. Brooks had it bad for her. Suggesting taking her to his room had been brash. Insane, really, since he'd known her less than an hour.

No one messes with Ruby unless she wants to be messed with.

Apparently he'd made the grade. 'Cause he was messing with her, and had her full approval.

He scooped her up from the bench, and she automatically wound her arms around his neck as he climbed the outside staircase that led to his room. She was petite and lightweight, and it wasn't a struggle to carry her up the stairs in his arms. Darkness concealed them for most of the way. Once he slid the key card into the lock and shoved the door open with a hip, he moved inside and set her on her feet. She still clung to him.

Lord have mercy.

They were finally alone. Brooks's deep sense of decorum kicked in big time. He knew what he was dealing with. She wasn't some floozy who staked men out in a bar. She wasn't an easy piece who'd consider him another conquest. He could tell that from the warm glow in her eyes now, from the way all the men at the bar respected her, from the way she'd chosen *him* and not the other way around. For all those reasons, he wasn't going to take advantage of the situation.

He brushed a kiss to her lips. "Welcome."

As antiquated as the inn was, at least the place was clean. There was no flat-screen television on the wall, no wet bar or cushy king-size bed for added luxury. Nor was there a spacious wardrobe closet or a sunken bathtub or any of the things Brooks was accustomed to. Ruby strolled over to peer out the back window. From where he stood, the view was hardly noteworthy or attractive: just a vast amount of unincorporated land. The lack of illumination was actually a plus since there was nothing to see out there. "I've never been inside one of these rooms," she said.

"I figured."

She whirled around. "You think you've got my number, Galahad?"

"Maybe. I know you don't do this."

Her bright laughter ended with an unfeminine snort. "You'd like to believe that, right?"

"I do believe it. So, why me?"

She glanced out the window again, gazing into the darkness. "Maybe I like you. Maybe it's because you came to my rescue—"

"Which you didn't need."

She continued, "You came to my rescue with no thought of the danger to your own hide."

He took a step toward her. "Are you saying I couldn't take that guy?"

"Hold on to your ego. I'm only saying that you're the one I want to be with tonight. Can't we leave it at that?"

He nodded and inclined his head toward the door.

"We were about to combust out there. That's never happened to me before."

"So, you're saying you don't like losing control and decided to slow down the pace?"

"What I'm saying is, you deserve better than that."

She smiled, and the natural sway of her body as she walked toward him fueled his juices. "There, you see? Things like that are exactly what a girl wants to hear. So, what did you have in mind?"

Her scent filled him up, and the shimmering sheet of dark, straight hair falling off her shoulders gave him pause—was he crazy to slow things down?

Her eyes were on him, warm and soft and patient.

"A drink, for starters?"

Another survey of the room had her gaze landing on the amber bottle of whiskey he'd brought from Chicago sitting on the bedside table. "Okay."

He grabbed two tumblers and poured the whiskey. The very best stuff. He'd figured he would need some fortification before meeting his biological father, but he'd never thought he would entertain a lady with it.

Standing before her, he offered her a glass. "Here you go."

She eyed the golden liquid. "Thanks. What should we drink to?"

"To unexpected meetings?"

She smiled. "I'm glad you didn't say 'to new beginnings.'"

He wouldn't. He wasn't in the market for a lover

or a girlfriend. And apparently, Miss Ruby—he didn't know her last name—wasn't looking for a relationship, either. She'd dropped enough hints about that tonight. Somebody must've hurt her along the way, but Brooks couldn't delve too deeply into her past. He wouldn't want anyone prying into his, and tonight was all about the present, not the past or the future.

He touched his glass to hers, and a definitive clink sounded in the room. "To unexpected *pleasant* meetings."

She gave him a brief nod and then took a sip, taking time to relish the taste before swallowing. "This is pretty amazing stuff. It surely didn't come out of any minibar."

He was surprised she would notice the quality. "Are you a whiskey expert?"

"Let's just say I know good whiskey when I taste it."

She took a seat on the bed and continued to sip. He sat beside her, enjoying her quiet company. His heart was still racing, but he was glad he'd toned things down some. She wasn't a woman to be rushed. And he wanted to savor her tonight, in the same way she was savoring her whiskey.

"Tell me," she said, "aren't you afraid that I'll come to my senses and walk out on you?"

"I don't think you're a flight risk, Ruby. So, no. But if you think better of this, I would respect your decision. When I make love to you, I want you to be sure and all in."

She smiled, and her eyes drifted down to the amber liquid in her glass. "You don't mince words."

"You don't, either."

She nodded, and her soft gaze met his stare. He reached out to touch her face with a sole finger to her cheek. She gasped, and a warm light flickered in her eyes.

"What do you want, Ruby?"

"Just a night," she whispered, breathy and guileless. "With you."

He sensed she needed it as much as he did. To have one night with her before his life would change forever.

Taking the glass from her and setting both of their drinks down on the nightstand, he cupped her face with his hands and gazed into her eyes. "One night, then."

"Yes," she said. "One night."

And then he pulled her up to a standing position so they were toe-to-toe, her face lifting to his. He peered into warm, dark eyes giving him approval and then slowly lowered his head, his mouth laying claim to hers.

Their night together was just beginning.

Two

Brooks's touch was like a jolt of electricity running the course of her body. One touch, one simple finger to her cheek, one slight meshing of his whiskey-flavored lips with hers, was giving her amnesia about the other men in her life. Men who'd trampled on her heart. Men like Trace, who'd taken from her and hadn't given back. Trace, the man she'd waited for all these months. She squeezed that notion from her mind.

Her time to wait was over.

Brooks's giving and patient mouth didn't demand. Instead, he encouraged her to partake and enjoy. She liked that about this man. He wasn't a player of women. No, her gladiator and presumptive keeper of her virtue was a man of honor. He didn't take. He gave. And that's exactly why she'd decided to come to his room tonight.

She placed her trust in him.

He wasn't asking her to bare her soul. But she would bare her body. For him.

Her fingers nimbly played with the tiny white buttons on her blouse until the material slipped from her shoulders, trapping her arms. Cool night air grazed her exposed skin.

Brooks's sharp intake of breath reached her ears. "You're unbelievably beautiful."

He worked the sleeves of her blouse down her arms until they gathered at her wrists. He held her there, mercilessly tugging her closer until her bra brushed his torso. "Yeah, I like you in red." He stroked her hair and then snapped the silky strap of her bra.

"It's my color," she whispered, and he smiled.

"I won't disagree."

He nipped at her lips then, several times, until his mouth claimed hers again. The kiss swept her into another world, where the only thing that mattered, all that she felt, was the pleasure he was giving. His tongue plunged in and met hers in a sparring match that ignited a fiery inferno within her. Whimpering, she ached for his touch. Finally his fingers dipped inside her bra to caress her nipples. Everything unfolded from there— the pleasure too great, the sighs too loud, the hunger too strong.

He worked magic with his mouth while his hands

found the fastener of her bra. Within seconds, and none too soon, she was free of her blouse and restraints. Her breasts spilled out into his awaiting hands, and the small ache at her core began to pulse as he touched, fondled and caressed her. She was pinned to the spot, unwilling to move, unwilling to take a step, his invisible hold on her body too strong. Her nipples stood erect and tightened to pebble hardness. Aching for more, she leaned way back and was granted the very tip of his tongue dampening her with moisture.

"Oh, so good, Brooks."

His outstretched palms bracing the small of her back, he answered only with a low guttural groan.

And once he was through ravaging her, he brought her up to eye level, drinking her in from top to bottom. Shaking his head, he fixed his gaze on the full measure of her breasts. She had a large bust for a petite woman and this time she didn't mind having a man's eyes transfixed on her. "I can't believe you," he muttered. "You're not real."

The compliment went straight to her head.

Brooks was a city dude, a man who didn't fit in her world, yet here she was, nearly naked with him and enjoying every sensual second of it.

"I'm very real," she breathed, closing the gap between them and lacing her arms around his neck. His erection stood like a stout monument, and there was no missing it. "And I want more."

"Whatever the lady wants," he said, running his

hands up and down the sides of her body, his finger-tips grazing the sides of her breasts. Another round of heat pinged her as anticipation grew.

He turned her around, came up behind her and slowly grazed the waistband of her jeans with his hands. His powerful arms locked her in, and his mouth was doing a number on her throat while his long fingers nudged her sweet spot. She murmured her approval, and lights flashed before her eyes. He stroked between her thighs, and a cry ripped from her throat. And then he was pull-ing the zipper of her jeans down, slowly, torturously, his erection behind her, a thrilling reminder of what was to come.

"Kick off your boots," he whispered in her ear.

Goose bumps erupted on her arms.

Her legs were a mass of jelly.

She kicked her boots off obediently, and then his index fingers were inside her waistband, gently lower-ing the jeans down her legs. She stepped out of them easily. "Red lace panties," he murmured appreciatively. He cupped one cheek, fitting her left buttock in his palm. He stroked her, smoothing his hand up and over, up and over. "Oh, man," he muttered, the heat of his body bathing her.

From where she stood with her back against his chest, she felt his body shudder. Quickly she turned around. The room was dimly lit with a sole lamp, and they were cast in shadow, but there was enough light to see a deep, burning hunger in his eyes.

"Lie down on the bed," he told her.

Her heart was pounding like a drum, beating hard, beating fast. He was a man who took control. She wasn't one to obey so easily, but there was a look in his eyes telling her to trust him. She did as she was told and lay on the queen bed, naked but for the panties she wore.

His gaze roamed over her body, slowly, the gleam in his eyes filled with promise.

"Galahad?"

"Hmm?"

"Having second thoughts?"

He laughed at her, giving his head a shake. "Are you kidding me? You have no idea…"

"What?"

"…how turned on I am. I'm trying to keep from jumping your bones, Ruby."

She glanced at the flagpole erection bulging in his pants. "What if I want you to jump my bones? Isn't that why we're here?"

He squeezed his eyes shut. "Yeah, but… I want this night to last."

She rolled to the side and leaned on her elbow. His eyes sought the spill of her hair touching her breasts. "Come to bed, Brooks. I'm a big girl. I can take whatever you have in mind."

"Doubtful, honey. What I'm thinking…"

She grabbed his hand and tugged. He landed on his butt in an upright position on the bed. "Do it, Brooks. But first take off your clothes."

He grinned. "How did I get so lucky?"

"Judging by the cut of your cloth, you were probably born lucky." She was guessing.

He grunted. And that was all the reply he gave her.

Sitting up on her knees, she helped him lift his shirt over his head and pull off his boots between kisses. Her hands sought his chest, all powerful and rippled with muscle, smooth and hard, like the planes of a solid board. She reveled in touching him, her fingertips toying with his flattened nipples.

That move landed her on her back, her arms locked by one strong hand above her head. "Two can tease," he said.

And then he was pulling her panties down and touching her where she'd prayed he'd touch. Her body instantly responded, and soft moans rose from her throat. She undulated with each stroke of his hand, each caress of a fingertip. He kept her pinned down, covering her with his body, the soft flesh of his palm applying pressure at the apex of her thighs.

"I'm… I'm going to lose it," she moaned, the pleasure unbearable.

"Don't fight it, honey," he rasped.

And then she shattered, and spasms wracked her lower body in beautiful jolts that electrified her body. Her hips were arched, and she didn't remember how they got that way. Slowly she lowered herself and finally opened her eyes to swim in Brooks's deep blue gaze.

He watched her carefully, a satisfied smile on his lips as he unzipped his pants and removed them.

"Your turn," she said.

He shook his head. "Our turn."

And then he fitted a condom on his erection and moved back over her.

His hands molded her breasts. His kiss went deep, his tongue delicious and probing. "Tell me when you're ready, sweetheart," he murmured before kissing her again.

She ran her hands through his longish blond hair, her fingers curling around the locks at the back of his neck. Then her gaze drifted to his eyes. "I don't think I'll ever be more ready."

He made a caveman sound, raw and brash, and then braced her in a protective way to roll them over on the bed. She found herself on top of him. "Set the pace, Ruby. I don't want to hurt you."

She bit the corner of her lip. Sure, she was petite, but Galahad worried that he was too big for her small frame. She could actually fall for a guy like this. She gave him a nod and straddled his thighs. "You won't hurt me," she said, fitting herself over his shaft, tossing her head back and shuddering from the feel of him inside her.

Then she began to move.

Spooned against Brooks's large frame, with his arm resting possessively around her torso, Ruby slowly opened her eyes. It was past midnight and she'd promised Brooks she'd stay the night with him. She didn't doubt her decision but instead smiled as he snuggled her closer and brought his hand to rest just under her breast.

"Are you awake?" he whispered, his breath warm on her neck.

"Just," she answered. "I dozed."

"Me, too. I haven't been this relaxed in a long time."

"Had a lot on your mind lately?" she murmured.

"You have no idea. But I don't want to talk about that right now."

His hand made lazy circles around her breast, his fingers feathery light over her nipple. Her body heated instantly. He had the ability to make her yearn, and the longing was potent. His leg moved over both of hers, and she was locked to him now, the soft flesh of her thighs meeting with legs of steel.

"I don't want to talk at all," he said, fisting her hair and planting kisses at the back of her neck. "Do you?"

"No." Oh God, what he was doing to her? Her body flamed. She was going up in smoke. "Talking is overrated. Not when we could be doing better things."

Ruby had never given herself so freely before. She'd never really been the *bad* girl, and everyone who knew her well knew that for a fact. She'd had only three relationships in her twenty-six years, and only the last one had really meant anything to her. The *last* one had hurt her.

She'd been in love.

Or so she'd thought.

But tonight with Brooks was different. It was all about having a man appreciate her. Give to her. Excite her and make her feel like a woman.

He rolled over on top of her, careful of her small frame, his hands bracing the bed on both sides of her head. She gazed into his deep blue eyes. "I want you again, Ruby."

Ruby smiled. "I want you, too."

He nodded and let go of a deep breath. "I was praying you'd say that, honey."

He bent his head and touched his mouth to hers. Already the taste of him, the firmness of his lips, seemed familiar and welcome. She'd never see him again. She wasn't in the market for a man. But Brooks would leave her with a good memory.

And then his mouth moved from her lips down her chest toward her navel, streaming kisses along the way. Her hips lifted; she was eager and willing, waiting. She didn't have to wait long. He touched his tongue to her center and suckled her sweetest spot. She whimpered and moved wildly as his mouth performed magic. It was a torturous, beautiful few minutes of pleasure. And when she was on the brink, ready for a powerful release, he rose over her and joined their bodies. Oh…it was bliss, the best of the best as he moved inside her. And then, moments later, his eyes darkened, his body stiffened and every sensation between them intensified. He moaned her name, an utterance of pleasured pain, and then he broke apart at the seams. It was enough to turn her inside out, and she, too, shuddered with an incredible release.

"Wow," she said once her breathing returned to normal.

"Yeah, wow," he said, keeping her close. He kissed her forehead, stroked her hair and tucked her body into his.

She closed her eyes and waited for the exquisite hum of her body to ease her into sleep.

Brooks tiptoed back into the room, holding two cups of coffee and a white paper bag filled with muffins and buttered biscuits from the café at the inn. There wasn't a croissant to be had in this hokey Texas town, and he liked that about this place. Clean, simple and... He glanced at Ruby asleep in the bed, her hair smooth black granite against the pillow. Beautiful. Yep, Cool Springs left him with a good impression.

The mattress groaned as he sat down.

"Is that coffee I smell?" a soft, sultry voice whispered from the other end of the bed.

"Can't fool you," he said, turning to find Ruby coming to a sitting position. "Leaded and dark as mud." Apparently that's how they made coffee in Texas. He showed her the two cups.

"I think I love you," she said, reaching for one. She'd worn one of his shirts to bed. The thing hung down to her knees and covered most of her up, but she still looked sexy as sin.

Her lips pursed as she blew on the rising steam.

He shook his head and talked down his lust. "Got biscuits, too, all buttered up, with honey."

"I adore you even more," she said. He handed her one and she wasted no time. She took a big bite, chewed with gusto and then took another bite.

"You've got an appetite."

"I had a busy day and *night*."

He joined in, sipping coffee and digging into the biscuits. "Maybe I should've taken you out for a nice big breakfast."

She shook her head. "This is perfect," she said, reaching for the bag from his hand. "What kind of muffins did you get?"

"Banana and blueberry. So, you wouldn't want to go out for breakfast with me?"

She chose blueberry. "It's nothing personal, but showing up somewhere public at this hour will cause talk. You know what they say about small towns. All of it is true. And you don't owe me anything, but I appreciate your gallantry."

"Just call me Galahad."

"I do." She laughed before putting her teeth into the muffin.

He laughed, too, and was sorry he had to leave Ruby behind. She wasn't like most females he'd met, and he had a feeling she wasn't going to put up a fuss about saying goodbye.

He wasn't entirely sure he liked that idea, but he had

a new life waiting for him. His emotions were keyed up, and he was too damn confused to add a woman to the mix.

They drank coffee and chatted quietly about nothing in particular. And after they'd taken their last sips, Brooks rose from the bed and began packing his belongings. "Sorry, but I have to hit the road soon. I have an important meeting."

Ruby rose from the bed and padded over to him. "Brooks," she said.

"Hmm?"

She stood before him, her expression unreadable. "Don't forget your shirt."

Slowly she began undoing the buttons, her nimble fingers working one after another. Once done, she shrugged out of the shirt, and it fell easily to her feet. His gaze fastened on a beautiful body in red lace. "Ruby," he said, sucking in oxygen and pulling her into his arms, her skin smooth and her muscles toned under his fingertips. "I wish I could postpone my meeting."

"No problem." Her eyes were soft and warm. He was never going to forget that particular deep cocoa color. Who was he kidding? He was never going to forget *her*. That was for damn sure. "I've got a busy day myself. I'll take a shower. You'll probably be gone by the time I get out."

Like a fool, he nodded. That was the plan. He had to leave. Now.

He claimed her lips one last time, putting all of himself into that kiss. Then, mustering every ounce of his willpower, he turned away from her. But a thought struck, and he reached into his pocket to pull out a business card. "In case," he said with a lift of his shoulder, "I don't know, if you want to talk. Or need me or something." He set the card on the bedside table.

By the time he turned back around, she had disappeared into the bathroom.

"Goodbye, Brooks," she said just as the door was closing.

The lock clicked.

He closed his eyes. It was time to get on with the rest of his life.

Three

Brooks pulled into the gates of Look Away Ranch, his gaze drawn to the size and scope of Beau Preston's horse farm. The animals grazing freely in white-fenced meadowlands had a majestic presence. They were tall, their coats gleaming in browns and blacks and golds. Brooks didn't know much about horses, but even an amateur could tell by looking at them that these stallions, mares and geldings were top-notch.

He smiled at the notion that the apple didn't fall far from the tree. If what he'd been told by Roman Slater, the PI he'd hired to find his biological father, was true, then Brooks's drive to succeed above all else must've been in his blood. Because Look Away Ranch had all the makings of hard-earned success, much like his very own Newport Corporation.

He, Graham and Carson had worked their asses off for years in order to create one of the leading real estate and land development companies in the country. He was proud of what they'd accomplished, coming up the real estate ranks in Chicago and becoming genuine competitors of Sutton Winchester's Elite Industries. Winchester was their biggest rival both professionally and privately. And Brooks had done his very best to take the ruthless older man down, more for personal reasons than professional.

For a time, Brooks had believed that the now ailing Sutton fathered him and his twin brother Graham. The knowledge only fueled his desire to destroy the man he believed abandoned his mother in her time of need, when she was pregnant. It turned out none of that was true. But paternity tests had revealed that his baby brother, Carson, was indeed Sutton Winchester's biological child. Sutton and his late mother, Cynthia, had history together. She'd been his secretary once, and they'd had a love affair.

He hoped his true father, Beau, would fill in the rest of the blanks. After years of wondering and months now of tracking the man down, Brooks was ready to meet the man who'd fathered him.

He pulled up into the portico-covered drive that circled the stately ranch house and killed the engine. A man was waiting on the steps. Brooks's first glimpse was of a tall rancher, his hair once blond and now dusted with silver, dressed in crisp jeans and a snap-down Western shirt. He immediately approached, marching down the steps, his gait extremely similar to his twin brother's and probably Brooks's as well. Warmth swamped his chest.

He was out of the car quickly, walking toward the man whose blood flowed through his veins. They came face-to-face, and Brooks took in the blue eyes, the firm jaw and the hint of a wicked smile bracing the man's mouth. "Beau?"

Tears welled in the man's eyes. His lips quivered and he nodded. "Yes, son. I'm Beau Preston. I'm your father."

His father's legs wobbled, and Brooks grabbed his shoulders to steady him. As emotion rocked him, Brooks's own legs went numb, too. Then his father broke down, sobbing quietly and taking Brooks into his big, sturdy arms as he would a little boy. "Welcome, son. Welcome. I've been searching for you for a long time."

A few seconds later, Beau backed away, wiping at his tears. "I'm sorry. I'm just so happy, boy. Come inside. We have a lot to talk about."

"Yes, I'd like that," Brooks said.

They walked shoulder to shoulder into the house.

"Forgive me for not showing you around just yet," Beau said.

"I understand. We have a lot of catching up to do."

But Brooks noticed things about the rooms he walked through, the sturdy, steady surroundings, dark wood floors polished to a mirror shine, bulky wood beams above and wide-paned windows letting the outside in. The wood tones were brightened by the red blooms of poinsettia plants placed in several of the rooms, and his nostrils filled with the holiday scent of pine.

His father led him into the great room, which contained a giant flat-screen television, a corner wet bar, and tan and black leather couches. He got the feeling this was his father's comfort zone, the room he relaxed in after a long, grueling day. "Have a seat," the older man said. "Can I offer you coffee or iced tea? Orange juice?"

Brooks had had morning coffee with Ruby. A slice of regret barreled through him that he'd never see her again. He sat down on a tan sofa. "No thanks. I'm fine."

"You found the place okay?" His father took a seat facing him, his gaze latching onto Brooks and gleaming as bright as morning sunshine. All of Brooks's apprehension over this meeting vanished. Beau was as glad they'd found each other as he was.

"Yep, didn't have any trouble finding Look Away Ranch. It's pretty amazing, I have to say."

"What's amazing is that you're finally here. And look at you, boy. You're the spitting image of me when I was your age."

"There are two of us, you know. But Graham wanted to lay back and let me make the first contact with you.

We didn't want to overwhelm you and, well…we have questions. He thought it'd be easier for you and me to speak privately before he joins us, since I was the one hell-bent on finding you."

His father rubbed at the back of his neck, a pained look entering his eyes. "I have to explain. I didn't know about you boys in the beginning. I didn't know your mama, Mary Jo, was carrying my babies when she ran away from Cool Springs. And once I started receiving anonymous notes and photos, I wasn't sure any of it was true, but as the photos kept coming, I saw the resemblance. It was unmistakable, and I moved heaven and earth to find Mary Jo. To find you boys."

"It's weird to hear you call my mother Mary Jo. As far as we knew, Mom's name was Cynthia Newport."

He shrugged a shoulder and got a faraway look in his eyes. "Mary Jo and I were desperately in love. She must've been scared out of her mind to run from me the way she did. That son of a bitch father of hers…" He paused to gauge Brooks's reaction. "Sorry, I forget he's your grandfather. But he was mean to the bone. Mary Jo was convinced if he found out she was seeing me, he'd kill both of us. I tried like the dickens to calm her down and tell her I'd protect her, but she must've panicked when she found out she was pregnant. God, I keep thinking how desperate she must've been back then. Alone in the world and carrying twins, no less. She wouldn't have run off if she wasn't terribly frightened of the consequences. That's all I can figure. She must've thought her daddy would beat the stuffing out of her, and harm her babies, if he ever found out the truth.

"I didn't know she'd changed her name and started a new life. I surely didn't know she was with child. But I want you to know, to be clear, I searched high and low for her in those early days. Trouble was, I was searching for Mary Jo Turner, not this…this Cynthia Newport person."

"I understand. I don't fault you for any of this. I've, uh, well, I'm just now coming to terms with all of this myself. I must admit, I was a bit obsessed with finding you."

"I'm glad you never let up, son."

Brooks gave him a nod. "Mom, she was a survivor. She did whatever it took to keep me and my brothers safe and cared for. She hid so many things from us during our lives. But Graham and I and our younger brother, Carson, who has a different father, don't blame her for any of it. We had a good life, living on the outskirts of Chicago with our Grandma Gerty. That woman befriended Mom when she was at a low point, and she took all of us in. She let us live with her in a modest home in a nice neighborhood, and she helped get us through school. We were a family in all respects. My brothers and I always looked upon her and loved her as if she was our real grandmother. I have a sneaking suspicion she was the one sending those updates and photos to you."

"Sounds like a wonderful woman." Beau sighed as he leaned farther back in his seat. "If she was the one, then I owe her a great debt. I'd long believed that your mother was gone to me forever, but just knowing you boys were out there somewhere gave me hope. I wish like hell Gerty would've just told me where to find you, but your mama probably held her to a promise to keep the secret."

"Grandma Gerty died about ten years ago."

"That's about when the updates stopped coming. It makes sense," his father said, "as much as any of this makes sense." He laughed with no real amusement.

"Grandma Gerty had a keen sense of duty. She must've believed in her heart she was doing the right thing. She only wanted what was best for my mom."

"I'm sorry Mary Jo isn't with us anymore. We were so young when we were in love, and…well, I have fond memories of her. Such a tragedy, the way she died."

"The aneurism took us all by shock. Mom was pretty healthy all of her life, and to lose her that way, after all she'd been through…well, it wasn't fair." Brooks took a second to breathe in and out slowly. After composing himself he added, "I miss her like crazy."

"I bet you do. The Mary Jo I remember was worthy of your love. I have no doubt she was a wonderful mother."

"Do you know what ever happened to my grandfather?"

"Still kicking. The mean ones don't die young. He's

in a nursing home for dementia patients and being cared for by the state of Texas. I'm sorry, son. I know he's your relation, but if you knew how he treated your mama, you wouldn't give him a second of thought."

Brooks closed his eyes. This part was hardest to hear. His mother had never mentioned her abuse to him or any of her children. She'd shielded them all from hurt and negativity and made their lives as pleasant and as full of love as she possibly could. She'd come to Chicago hell-bent on changing her circumstances, but those memories of her broken youth must've haunted her. To think of her as that young girl who'd been treated so poorly by the one person who should've been loving and protecting her burned Brooks like a hot brand. "I suppose I should visit him."

"You can see him, son. But I'm told he's lost his mind. Doesn't recognize anyone anymore."

Brooks nodded. Another piece of his family lost to him. But perhaps in this case it was for the best that his grandfather wouldn't know him. "I'll deal with him in my own way at some point."

"I'm glad you agreed to stay on at the ranch awhile. You're welcome at the house. It's big enough and always open to you. But when we spoke on the phone, you seemed to like the idea of staying at the cabin right on our property and…well, I think it's a good choice. You can take things at your own pace without getting overwhelmed." His father grinned and gave his head a prideful tilt. "Course, here I am talking about you getting overwhelmed when you're the owner of a big corporation and all."

Brooks grinned. That apple not falling far from the tree again. "And here you are with this very prosperous horse farm in Texas. You have a great reputation for honesty and quality. Look Away Ranch is top-notch." Aside from having Beau Preston investigated by Slater, Brooks had Googled him and found nothing lacking.

"It's good to hear you say that. Look Away has been a joy in my life. I lost my wife some years ago, and this place along with my sons helped me get through it. You'll meet your half brothers soon."

"I'll look forward to that. And I'm sorry to hear about you losing your wife."

"Yeah, it was a tough one. I think you would've liked her. I know Mary Jo would've approved. My Tanya was a good woman. She filled the hole inside me after losing your mama."

"I wish I could've known her, Beau."

His eyes snapped up. "Son, I'd appreciate it if you called me Dad."

Dad? A swell of warmth lodged deep in his heart. He'd never had the privilege of calling any man that. While growing up, he, Carson and Graham had always been the boys without a father. Grandma Gerty had made up for it in many ways, her brightness and light shining over them, but deep down Brooks had wanted better answers from his mother about his father's absence in their lives. "You're better off not knowing," she'd say, cutting off his further questions.

Brooks gave Beau a smile. "All right, *Dad*. I'm happy to call you that after all these years."

His father's eyes lit up. "And I'm happy to hear it, son. Would you like to get settled in? I can drive you to the cabin. It's barely more than a stone's throw from here, only a quarter mile into the property."

"Yeah, that's sounds good."

"Fine, and before we do, I'll give you the grand tour of the house. Tanya did all the decorating and she loved the holidays, so we've kept up the tradition of putting out all her favorite things. We start early in December, and it takes us a while to bring the trees in and get the house fully decorated in time for our annual Look Away Ranch Christmas shindig. C'mon, I'll show you around now."

"Thanks. I've got no doubt I'm going to like your place."

"I hope so, son."

After his father left him at the cabin, a rustic, wood-beamed, fully state-of-the-art three-bedroom dwelling that would sell for a million bucks in the suburbs of Chicago, Brooks walked his luggage into the master suite and began putting away his belongings in a dark oak dresser. Lifting out the shirt Ruby had worn just this morning, Brooks brought the collar to his nose and breathed in. The shirt smelled of her still, a wildly exotic scent that had lured him into his best fantasy to date.

He'd hold on to that memory for a long time, but now he was about to make new ones with his father and his family. Brooks walked the rooms, getting familiar with his new home—for the next few weeks, anyway—and found he was antsy to learn more, to see more.

He grabbed a bottle of water from the fridge, noting that Beau Preston didn't do things halfway. The fridge was filled with everything Brooks might possibly need during his stay here. If Beau wanted him to feel welcome, he'd succeeded.

Locking the cabin door with the key his dad had given him, he headed toward the stables to explore. What he knew about horses and ranching could fit in his right hand, and it was about time to change that. Brooks didn't want to admit to his father he'd seen the saddle side of a horse only once or twice. What did a city kid from Chicago know about riding?

Not much.

Huddled in a windbreaker jacket fit for a crisp December day in Texas, his boots kicking up dust, he came upon a set of corrals first. Beautiful animals frolicked, their groomed manes gently bouncing off their shoulders as they played a game of equine tag. They nipped at each other, teased and snorted and then stormed off, only to return to play again. They were beauties. *His father's horses.*

The land behind the corrals was rich with tall grazing grass, strong oaks and mesquite trees dotting the squat hills. It was unfamiliar territory and remote, uniquely different from what Brooks had ever known.

He ducked into one of the stables. Shadows split the sunshine inside, and a long row of stalls on either side led to a tack room. The stable was empty but for a dozen or so horses. Beau had told him to check out Misty, an eight-year-old mare with a sweet nature. He spotted her quickly, a golden palomino with blond locks, not too different in color from his own.

"Hey, girl, are you and I going to get along?" The horse's ears perked up, and she sauntered over to hang her head over the split door. "That's a girl." He stroked the horse's nose and looked into her big brown eyes. "Hang on a sec," he said and walked over to the tack area. The place smelled of leather and dust, but it was about as clean and tidy as a five-star hotel.

That told him something about his father.

"Can I help you?" A man walked out of the tack room and eyed him cautiously. "I'm Sam Braddox, the foreman."

Brooks put out his hand. "I'm Brooks Newport. Nice to meet you."

The man's expression changed to a quick smile. "You're one of Beau's boys."

"Yes, I am. I just got here a little while ago."

"Well, welcome. I see the resemblance. You have your daddy's eyes. And Beau only just this morning filled the crew in on the news you'd be arriving."

"Thanks. I'm... I'm just trying to get acquainted with the place. Learn a little about horses." He scratched his head and then shrugged. "I'm no horseman, but Beau wants to take me out riding one day."

Sam studied him. "How about a quick lesson?"

"Sure."

"C'mon. I'll show you how to saddle up." He led Misty out of her stall and into an open area.

"Misty's a fine girl. She's sweet, but she can get testy if you don't show her who's boss from the get-go."

"Okay."

The foreman grabbed a worked-in saddle and horse blanket and walked over to Brooks. "Here we go."

Sam tossed the blanket over the horse just as one of the crew dashed in. "Hey, Boss. Looks like Candy is ready to foal. She's having a struggle. Brian sent me to get you."

"Okay." Sam sighed. "I'll be right there." He gave Brooks a glance and set the saddle on the ground. "Sorry about this. Candy has had a hard pregnancy. I'd better get right to it."

"No problem at all. I'll see you later, Sam."

"You okay here?"

"I'm gonna try my hand at it. I'll Google how to saddle a horse."

Sam gave him a queer look. "All right." Then he strode out like his pants were on fire.

"How hard can this be?" Brooks said to himself.

He fixed the blanket over the horse's shoulders,

sheepskin side down, and then lifted the saddle. The darn thing weighed at least fifty pounds. He set it onto the horse and grabbed the cinch from underneath the horse's belly.

"You're doing it all wrong." The female voice stopped him short. What in hell? He whipped around, uneasy about where his thoughts were heading. Sure enough, there was Ruby of his fantasies coming forward. His mouth could've dropped open, but he kept his teeth clamped as he tried to make sense of it. He'd just left Ruby a few hours ago, and now here she was in the flesh, appearing unfazed at seeing him again. He, for sure, wasn't unaffected.

"Ruby?"

"Hello, Brooks."

She practically ignored him as she went about removing the saddle like a pro—a saddle that weighed probably half her body weight—and shoving it into his arms. "The blanket has to be even on both sides. You put it on closer to Misty's shoulders and then slide it into the natural channel of her body. Make sure it's not too far down on her hips, either. It's the best protection the horse has for—"

"Ruby?" He took hold of her arm gently.

She didn't budge, didn't face him. "I work here. I'm Look Away Ranch's head wrangler and horse trainer."

As if that explained it all. "Did you know who I was last night?"

Her eyes snapped up. "God, no." She shook her head,

and the sheet of beautiful raven hair shimmered. "Beau told us about you only this morning. He wanted to make sure you were really coming before he shared his news. Welcome to the family, Brooks."

His heart just about stopped. "The family?"

She nodded. "Beau's like a father to me."

Brooks released the breath he'd been holding. She'd had him scared for a second that they could be related in some way. "Like a father? What does that mean?"

"My father worked for Beau all of his life, until he died ten years ago. I was sixteen at the time. It was hard on me. I, uh…it almost broke me. My dad was special to me. We both loved horses, the land and everything about Look Away, so when he passed, I couldn't imagine my life without him. But Beau and his boys were right by my side the entire time. Beau never let a day go by without letting me know I was welcome and wanted here. He took me in and I worked at Look Away, making my way up to head wrangler."

"You live here?"

"I have an apartment in town, but often I stay in the old groundskeeper's cottage, especially during the holidays. It's where my dad lived out the last years of his life. It's home to me, too, and Beau's family is now my family."

Brooks nodded at this new wrinkle in his life. "What about your mother?"

"Mom died when I was very young. I don't remember too much about her."

"I'm sorry." He put his hands on his hips. "So, what do we do now?"

"Now?" Her brows knit together. "What do you mean?"

"About us?"

Her olive skin turned bright pink, and her embarrassment surprised him. The Ruby he'd met yesterday had been fearless and uninhibited. "Oh, that. Well, it'd be best if we didn't discuss what happened between us last night. Beau wouldn't approve. It was really nice, Brooks. But not to be repeated."

"I see."

"Glad you do," she said, dismissing the subject with a flip of her hair. "You want to learn how to saddle this horse correctly?"

Dumbfounded, he began nodding, not so much because he gave a damn about saddling, but because Ruby living on his father's ranch blew his mind. "Uh, sure."

"Okay, so the blanket has to be even and protecting the horse from the saddle." Next this petite five-foot-something of a woman positioned the heavy saddle on her knee. "Put the stirrups and straps over the saddle seat so you don't hit the horse or yourself by accident when you're saddling up. Now use your leg for support and then knee it up in a whipping motion like this." With the grace of a ballerina, she heaved the weighty saddle onto the horse's back. "You want the saddle up a little high on the shoulders first, then slowly go with the grain of the horse's hair to slide it into place. This way you won't cause any ruffle to the hair that might irritate the horse later on. Proper saddling should cause your mount no harm at all. Doing it wrong can cause all kinds of sores and injuries."

"Got it."

Ruby gave Misty several loving pats on the shoulder. She spoke kindly to the animal, as one would to a friend, and the horse stood stock-still while she continued with a ritual she probably did every day.

Ruby adjusted the front cinch strap. "Make sure it's not too loose or too tight. Just keep tucking until you run out of latigo. Take a look at how I did this one and you do the back one."

"Okay, will do." He made a good attempt at fastening the cinch, Ruby standing next to him. His concentration scattered as she brushed up against him to fix the cinch and buckle it.

"Not bad, Brooks. For your first try."

Her praise flattered him. And her sweet scent filtering up to his nose blocked out the stable smells.

"Now that Misty is saddled, you want to make sure all buckles are locked in and all your gear is in good shape. Here's a trick. Slide your hand under the saddle up front." She placed her small hand under the blanket and saddle. "If your hand goes under with no forcing, you're good to go and you know your horse isn't being pinched tight. Isn't that right, Misty?"

As she stroked Misty's nose, the horse responded with a turn of her head. The two were old pals, it seemed. Ruby's big brown eyes lifted to him. "If you want some pointers on riding, I've got some time."

Mentally he winced. He had trouble focusing. He kept thinking about Ruby in his bed. Ruby naked. Ruby making love to him. Feisty, fierce Ruby. He should back away and make an excuse. Gain some perspective. But she was offering him something he needed.

Just like last night.

"Yeah, show me what you've got."

She stared at him for a beat of a second, her face coloring again. They were locked into the memory of last night, when she'd shown him what she had. And it was not to be equaled. "Stop saying stuff like that, Brooks. And we'll do just fine."

It was good to know that she wasn't as unaffected as she wanted him to believe.

"Right. All I can promise is I'll try."

Once Brooks was away from the stable and on horseback, Ruby could breathe again. She'd never expected her one-time, one-night fling to end up being Beau Preston's long-lost son. The irony in that was killing her.

"You're not a bad rider, Brooks," she said to him.

"I'll take that as a compliment." He tipped the hat she'd given him to wear. He didn't look half bad in a Stetson.

"Actually, you learn fast. You saddled up my horse pretty darn well."

"If you're trying to butter me up, it's working, honey."

"Just speaking the truth. And can you quit the endearments?"

He smiled. "You don't like me calling you honey?"

"I'm not your honey, Brooks. Ruby Lopez never has been anyone's honey." Except for Trace's at one time, but the sweetness of the term had soured along with the relationship.

They rode side by side along a path that wound around the property. She wanted out of this conversation. Brooks didn't need to know about her lack of a love life. But for some reason, when he was around, she did and said things she normally wouldn't.

"Ruby?"

"Hmm."

"I find that hard to believe. There's been no one in your life?"

"No one I care to talk about."

"Ah, I thought so. You've been burned before. The guy must be a loser."

"He isn't." Why on earth was she defending Trace?

"Must be, if he hurt you."

"Remember what I told you? When you want the horse to stop, pull back on one rein. Not two. Two can toss you forward, and that's a fight you can't win."

"Yeah, I remember, but why—"

"See you later, Brooks!" Ruby gave Storm Cloud a nudge, and the horse fell into a gallop. The ground rumbled underneath her stallion's hooves, and she leaned back and enjoyed the ride, grinning.

She thought she'd left Misty and her rider in the dust, but one quick look back showed her she was wrong. Brooks wasn't far behind, encouraging Misty to catch up. Ruby had five lengths on them, at best. But it wasn't a race. She couldn't put Brooks in danger. For all his courage and eagerness to learn, he was still a novice. "Whoa, slow up, Cloud." A slight tug on the rein was all that was needed. Cloud was a gem at voice commands. Beau had given her Storm Cloud on her eighteenth birthday, and she'd trained him herself. They were simpatico.

Brooks caught up to her by a copse of trees and came to a halt. "Is that your way of changing the subject?" His mouth was in a twist.

She shrugged a shoulder. "I don't know what you mean."

"Cute, Ruby."

"Hey, I'm impressed you caught up."

"Because you let me."

"Okay, I let you. But I couldn't endanger Beau's long-lost son."

"*One* of his sons. I've got a twin brother."

"Oh, no. There are two of you?" She smiled at him. This morning Beau had briefed her on all the sad events of his early life. He'd lost the woman he loved and his twins when she ran away from her abusive father. It was something Ruby had heard rumored, but it was never really spoken about in the Preston household.

"Yeah, I'm afraid so."

She tilted her head. "Can the world handle it?"

"The world likes the Newport brothers for the most part. But the question is, can you handle it?"

"I already told you, I'm good with you being here."

"I might be staying quite a while."

It was time to set him straight, and she hoped to heaven she could heed her own warning. "You're a city guy who's out of place in the country. You run a big company, and I'm at home in a barn. You're also the son of my best friend and mentor. The man is almost a father to me. You'd better believe I can handle it. There's no other option, Brooks."

He gave her a nod, his mouth turning down. "You're right. But when I look at you and remember..."

"Don't look at me."

"You're hard to miss, honey."

Honey again? "It's time to head back." She didn't wait for his reply. She turned Storm Cloud around. "Let's go, Cloud." With a slight nudge of the stirrup, the horse took off in a canter.

"I didn't peg you for a runner," Brooks called out.

But that's exactly what she was.

This time.

With this man.

She wasn't lying. She had no other choice.

Four

"You're cooking?" Brooks asked Ruby as he walked into his father's kitchen later that day.

Ruby glanced at him from her spot at the stove. She wore a black dress that landed just above her knees, fitting every curve on her body like a glove. A pink polka-dotted apron tied at the neck and waist didn't detract from the look. Brooks was beginning to think Ruby looked sexy in everything she wore.

"I'm cooking. Beau wanted me to make you a special dinner for your first night here."

"Do you cook every night?"

"No, that's Lupe's job. She's the best cook in the county, but this recipe comes from my father's family, and it's something Beau likes me to cook on occasion."

Brooks walked over to the stove. "I'm the occasion?"

She smiled. "You're the occasion."

He lifted the top off the enamel pot. Steam drifted up, and the scents of Mexico filled the room.

"Be careful. It's hot," she said, shoving a pot holder into his hand.

"What is it?"

"It's called *receta de costillas de res en salsa verde*. It's braised short ribs in tomatillo sauce."

"Smells delicious."

"It's not too spicy for a gringo." Her mouth twisted.

"You're all the spice I can manage in his house."

Ruby whipped her head around to the kitchen door. "*Dios!* Don't say things like that," she whispered. "I don't like lying to Beau."

"How did you lie?"

"It was a lie of omission. I didn't tell him I've already met you."

She'd met him and slept with him. And Brooks was having a hard time forgetting it. "He won't hear it from me, Ruby." He wasn't a kiss-and-tell kind of man. "I'm starving. Can I have a taste?" he asked.

"I suppose."

She grabbed a fork and dipped it into the stew. The meat she pierced fell easily away, and she lifted the steamy forkful up to his mouth. "Here. Tell me if it needs anything."

Brooks looked into her dark brown eyes as she fed him a morsel. The heat on the stove didn't compare to how he was heating up just being close to Ruby again. And then he began to chew. The seasoned meat blasted his palate with savory goodness. "Mmm. The lady can toss a man over her shoulder, ride a horse like nobody's business *and* cook."

"So, you like it?"

He nodded and stepped inches closer to her. "Is there anything you don't do well?" She didn't back away, and he didn't bother pretending he wasn't talking about her prowess in the bedroom.

She nibbled on her lower lip. "Brooks."

He ignored her warning tone, sensing she was as caught up as he was. He leaned forward and focused on her tempting mouth.

"Well, I see you've met Ruby already, Brooks."

The booming voice startled him, and he quickly stepped away. Ruby turned back to the stove, and Brooks answered his father. "Yes, I've met Ruby. She was kind enough to give me a taste of her stew."

Beau nodded. "It's a favorite of mine. I figured you might like it, too."

He bypassed Brooks to give Ruby a gentle kiss on the cheek. "Ruby's like a daughter to me." He gazed warmly into her eyes, and Ruby gave him a sweet, affectionate smile. "She's been with us since she was a tot. Her daddy was foreman around here, and Ruby grew up at the Look Away for all intents and purposes. I don't think there's a better horse wrangler in all of Texas, and everybody knows it."

"Thank you," she said.

"Actually, Ruby and I went for a ride this afternoon," Brooks said, to add something to the conversation.

"Good, good." Beau beamed with pride. "I want you to feel comfortable on Look Away. Did Ruby teach you a few things?"

Brooks met her eyes. "More than a few things."

The feisty Latina with the killer body blushed and put her head down to stir the stew, avoiding eye contact with him altogether now. It was clear this meal was going to be awkward, to say the least.

"My boys—your half brothers—will join us another night," Beau commented. "They're giving us time to get better acquainted. I hope you don't mind it'll just be you and me. And Ruby, of course."

"I can give you two time alone, too, Beau," Ruby jumped in, obviously trying to remove herself from the situation.

"I won't hear of it," Beau said. "Not after you cooked all afternoon for us. You're gonna sit right down and enjoy the meal along with us, Ruby. You work too hard as it is. Tonight we're gonna relax and get to know Brooks."

Ruby's gaze dimmed, and Brooks hid his amusement, but somehow Ruby knew he was laughing at her. From behind Beau's back, she gave him the stink eye.

Now that she was at the ranch, he couldn't imagine keeping away from her. Not touching her again was messing with his mind. He had bigger problems, but the idea of delicate, petite Ruby Lopez sitting by his side at dinner had him tied up in knots.

She was about as off-limits as a woman could get.

Brooks had never run from a challenge in his life, as old man Sutton Winchester could testify.

But Brooks was used to getting what he wanted in life.

And he was beginning to think Ruby was all that and more.

Once they were seated at the table and diving into the food, Beau asked, "So, what do you think about the ranch so far? Seeing it on horseback is a good way to gain perspective on the property, son."

Son? Would there ever come a day when Brooks would tire of hearing his father call him that? For so many years, Brooks had wondered what it would be like to know his true father, to sit down with him and have a meal. Now he was living the reality, and it all seemed surreal. "It's…it's a great spread, pretty impressive."

"And I bet Ruby picked out a good horse for you to ride."

"He rode Misty," she said.

"Ah, good," Beau said, nodding. It was the horse Beau had suggested.

"You know, Brooks, Ruby learned from the best. Her daddy, Joaquin, was my foreman and head wrangler for many years." Beau's eyes once again touched on Ruby with affection. "It'd make me real proud and happy if you'd think of Ruby as family, son. I mean, once you two get better acquainted."

Ruby's olive skin flushed with color. She immediately scraped her chair back, rose from her seat and went over to open the refrigerator. "I forgot the iced tea," she mumbled.

Beau ran a hand down his face and gave his head a shake. "Uh, sorry, honey. I forget how independent you are. I didn't mean to make you uncomfortable."

"You didn't," she said, pouring tea into three glasses, her back to them. "I'm fine, Beau."

Brooks's gaze dipped to her rear end in that tight-fitting dress, her long hair falling down her back like a sheet of black silk. He wasn't about to touch upon this subject, so he stayed silent. His father's request only cemented his need to keep far away from Ruby, which wasn't going to be easy since they'd be living on the ranch together now. Every time he laid eyes on the woman, something clicked inside his head. And way farther south.

Shelve those thoughts, man.

She came back to the table, delivered the drinks and scooted back into her chair.

"Thanks," Brooks said.

"You're welcome," she said, giving him a quick smile.

"Yeah, thanks honey. Meal's real delicious."

"Yes," Brooks added. "You're a talented cook, Ruby."

Among other things.

* * *

Ruby escaped the dinner early, claiming a case of fatigue and a desire for Beau to get to know Brooks on a one-on-one basis. Beau was ecstatic to have his son finally home. She saw it in his eyes, heard it in his tone. And she was truly happy for him. He'd told her he'd been haunted for years, had searched for and lamented the loss of the children he knew were out there somewhere. Now he'd been given a second chance to father them and bring them into the family.

Twins, no less.

Dios, it was weird having Brooks here. He made her nervous, and she couldn't say that about too many things. She was a woman who usually didn't go in for one-night flings, yet the one time she'd indulged, fate pulled a fast one on her by bringing Brooks right to her doorstep. Weren't one-night stands supposed to be just that—secret liaisons that both parties could walk away from?

She needed to purge thoughts of Brooks Newport Preston. He'd taken up too much space in her mind today. She made a detour and walked the path to the stables. Checking in on her horses always made her feel better.

One peek inside the dimly lit stable told her all was right in the horse world at Look Away. Beau bred dozens of horses to sell, and it was her job to make sure they were healthy and happy and well-trained. She knew enough not to form an emotional attachment to most of them. She knew not to love them, because that bond was sure to be broken as soon as the sale became final. Her papa had warned her enough times when she was a young girl, and after a few pretty brutal heartbreaks, she'd learned that lesson the hard way. Now Ruby knew when to love and when not to love.

Unfortunately she hadn't been that astute when it came to men.

But the horses in this stable weren't in danger of being sold off. They all belonged to the Preston family, except for Storm Cloud. He was all hers.

"Hey, Cloud," she whispered, tiptoeing to his stall. "You still up?"

Cloud wandered over to her, his head coming over the split door to say hello with a gentle nudge. "Yes, you are." Ruby stroked the side of his face, pressing a kiss above his nose. The horse gave a little snort, and Ruby chuckled. "You want a treat, don't you?"

She grabbed her secret stash from a bag hooked on the wall and came up with a handful of sugar cubes. "Only a few," she said. "And let's be quiet about it. Or the others will wake up."

Cloud gobbled them within seconds, and Ruby spent a few more minutes with him before she said goodnight. Feeling better, she walked toward the cottage she called home while she was staying on the Look Away. Carrie Underwood's "Before He Cheats" banged out of her phone, and she glanced at the screen.

Trace?

Her heart sped up. Why was he calling now, of all times? He hadn't had the balls to call her for six months. She'd invested almost two years in him, mainly during the off-season of the rodeo. They'd dated and had an amazing time together. But it wasn't all fun and games on her part. She'd fallen hard for the bull rider, giving him something she'd always protected and kept safe— her heart. Yet when the rodeo started up again this year, he'd left her high and dry. He hadn't called. He hadn't written. A few texts in the beginning, and that had been it, for heaven's sake. She'd spent the first months making excuses for him because the rodeo was an important part of his life. He was busy. He was focused on making a name for himself. But in the end, Ruby came to the conclusion that Trace had not only tried to make a name for himself but also made a damn fool out of her.

Carrie Underwood was about to carve her name in her guy's leather seats, and Ruby had a mind to do that very thing to Trace's truck if she ever saw him again. But her curiosity got the better of her. Before her cell went to voice mail, she answered the call.

"Hello."

"Ruby? Baby, is that you? It's Trace."

"I know who it is, Trace. Are you bleeding or on your last breath or something?"

Silence for a few seconds, and then, "No, baby. I'm not. What I *am* is missing you."

"You're not dying and trying to ease your conscience?"

"Ruby, listen to me. I know it's been a while."

"A while? Is that what you call six months of deafening silence? Why are you calling me now, Trace?"

"I told you, babe. I miss you like crazy. It's been hell on the circuit and I couldn't think straight, so I had to close off my mind to everything but what I was trying to accomplish. I needed the space to keep my head in the game. You can ask anybody around here. They all know about you, baby. They're sick of me pining for you. They all know I'm crazy about you."

Ruby's heart dipped a little. Trace was saying all the right things. He had charm and dark dastardly good looks. His voice, that deep Southern drawl, could melt an iceberg. But her wounds were deep, and she wasn't through being mad at him. "Not good enough, Trace. I'm sorry. I've got to go."

"Ruby, baby…wait."

"I have, Trace. For too long. Good night."

She pushed End and then squeezed her eyes shut. Pain burned through her belly, and those old feelings she'd managed to bury threatened to bust their way back up and slash her again and again.

He's like the horse I wasn't supposed to love.

Dios, why did he have to call her tonight?

She didn't want to think about him anymore.

Carrie's voice carried the same tune again, Ruby's cell phone drowning out the night sounds and coyote calls. No, damn it. She wasn't going to answer her phone again. No matter how many times Trace called. Her finger was ready to push the end button again. Until she saw the name flashing on the screen.

Serena.

Oh, thank goodness. She picked up quickly.

"Serena, hi," Ruby said anxiously. "I'm glad you called. You must've been reading my mind."

"Ruby, wow. Is everything all right? You sound stressed."

"I just got a call from Trace. And yeah, I'm a little stressed. I need to talk to you."

"Tell me. I'm listening."

"Oh boy, it's almost too much to explain over the phone. Can we meet for lunch tomorrow?"

"Of course, sure. That's the reason I was calling anyway. I wanted to catch up with you. It's been weeks since I've seen you. I miss my friend."

"I miss you, too. And there's a *whole lot* to catch up on. I'm buying. Root beer floats and sliders at the diner sound okay?"

"I won't pass up that offer. I'll see you there at noon."

Ruby sighed. Her bestie from high school was the only one she could confide in. "Thank you. I don't know what I'd do without you." Ruby didn't have a mom or an aunt or anyone female in her family she could talk to. Without Serena, she'd have been lost. Ever since they were kids, they'd shared their secrets with each other. Ruby ended the call, feeling a little better about things. Just knowing Serena would listen and not judge her made all the difference in the world. Though they didn't share bloodlines, they were sisters in all other respects. She'd relied on Serena's friendship to see her through some of the really tough times in her life.

"I'm eager to show you around Look Away, Brooks. Mind if we saddle up after breakfast and take us a ride?" Beau asked on Brooks's second morning on the ranch. "I'd love for you to see our operation."

"Uh, sure. I'd like that," he said, setting aside his coffee cup and patting his belly. "If I won't break poor Misty's back after the giant meal I just consumed. It was delicious, Lupe. I ate up everything in sight." Breakfast had included maple-smoked bacon, ham, eggs, chile-fried potatoes and homemade biscuits with gravy. "If I keep eating like this, I'll be as big as this house, but smiling all the way."

Lupe gave him a nod. "*Gracias*, Brooks. I'm happy to cook for Beau's son."

"Lupe is a triple threat to all of us. Breakfast, lunch and dinner. We have to work out hard around here to avoid putting the pounds on."

Beau's eyes were on him—the blue in them the exact same hue as his own—and he was beaming. Having his father look at him that way humbled him and made him feel as if he belonged. Even though ranch living was foreign to Brooks, it felt damn good knowing he was welcomed and—yes—loved by this obviously decent, successful and well-respected man.

A sudden case of guilt spilled into his good mood.

Would Beau approve of the tactics he'd used to bring Sutton Winchester down? Brooks hadn't taken any prisoners on that score, too eager to exact his revenge on the man he believed had immeasurably hurt his mother and his family. Brooks had looked upon Sutton as his enemy and hadn't held back, using all the tools at his disposal to get back at the dying man.

But was Sutton the monster he'd made him out to be? Or had he simply protected his mother's secrets at her urging, thus refusing to reveal who Cynthia really was? Had Sutton truly loved his mother enough to withstand all the media and personal attacks Brooks had thrown his way? It was hard thinking of Sutton in softer terms, as a man who'd go the distance for a woman to protect her. Everything else about Winchester pointed to him being a ruthless bastard.

Brooks was still sorting this all out in his mind.

"Son?"

Beau was on his feet, waiting for him.

"Yep, I'm ready, Dad." His lips twitched, and suddenly he felt like a child being given an unexpected gift. He had a sense that Beau was feeling that way, too, as they walked out of the kitchen, ready to take a ride together as father and son.

Minutes later, Brooks had saddled up and mounted Misty. Beau was atop a stunning black gelding named Alamo. "I figured you'd be a fast learner. You saddled up that mare almost perfectly."

Brooks lowered the brim of his hat and nodded at

his father's praise. "Thanks. The truth is, I don't know much about horses. I don't get out of the city much. My friend Josh Calhoun owns a dairy farm in Iowa, and that's about the only time I've seen the backside of a horse. Let me tell you, it wasn't pretty."

Beau chuckled. "I think I learned to ride before I could walk, son. You'll get the hang of it, and if you need any help, just ask me or Ruby. She's actually the expert. She's got the touch, you know."

He knew.

"That girl can tame the most stubborn of animals."

Beau went on to explain that in the summer months, Ruby gave lessons to children three mornings a week, teaching them how to respect and care for the animals. "It's a sight to see. All those kids swarming around her, asking her questions. Anyone who knows Ruby knows she's not the most patient kind. She likes things to get done, the faster the better, as long as they're done right. But Ruby, with those kids…well, it's my favorite time of year, watching her school those young kids."

Ruby with kids? Now that was an image that entered Brooks's head and lingered.

They rode out a ways, Beau showing him all the stables and corrals and training areas. There were out-buildings and supply sheds and feed shacks on the property. They rode along the bank of a small lake and then over flatlands that bordered the property. Beau's voice filled with pride when he spoke of his land and the improvements he'd made on the horse farm through the years.

"Enough about me, son. I want to hear all about you and your brothers. And your life in Chicago."

"Where do I start?"

"From the beginning…as you remember it."

"Well, let's see. Going back to my earliest years, Mom was always there for us. We lived with Mom's best friend, an older widow named Gerty, as you know. She was Grandma Gerty to us, and there wasn't a day that went by that my brothers and I didn't feel loved. As adults, we found out what a truly generous woman she was. She put a roof over our heads, raised us while Mom was working and helped all three of us get through college."

Brooks sighed, relieved. "That's good to hear, son."

"We had a good life, but all throughout growing up, Mom always told us we were better off that our father wasn't in our lives. I guess that was Mom's way of protecting us. And you, as well. I'm guessing she feared her fake identity would be discovered. Gosh, her father must've really done a number on her."

Beau's brows pushed together, and his scowl said it all. "You don't want to know."

Brooks nodded. Maybe he didn't.

He went on. "While she was pregnant, she worked for Sutton Winchester as his personal secretary. They fell in love, and she must've shared her secret with him about her life and the true father of her twins. I think

he protected her secret all those years, and then things
went bad between them. His ex was making all kinds
of trouble, and Mom walked away, but by then, she was
pregnant with Carson."

"It's quite a story."

"I know, but all through it, Mom was our constant. I
miss her so much. But I will admit to being angry with
her, with you, with Winchester. I became obsessed with
learning the truth."

"Good thing, or we would've never found each other,
son."

"That much is true. But I'm pretty relentless when I
go after something."

"You saying you have regrets?"

He shrugged. "Maybe. But not about coming here
and being with you, Dad."

Sitting tall in the saddle, riding the range with his
father and learning about Look Away all seemed sort
of right to him. Though he had a full life in Chicago, a
successful business to run and family he could count
on, being in Texas right now gave him a sense of belonging that he'd not had for a long time.

"I think we all have regrets," Beau said. "I shouldn't
have stopped until I found Mary Jo. Gosh, son, you have
to know how much losing her ate me up inside. After a
time, I really thought she was dead. And I blamed her
old man for it. He's a shell of what he once was, but I
never knew a meaner man."

"He must've been for my mom to run from you and

her hometown, the only place she'd ever lived. Only goes to show how strong my mother was."

"And brave, Brooks. I don't know too many women who would be able to assume a new identity, get a job, raise her boys and give them a life filled with love. Mary Jo was something."

"Yeah, Mom was that."

As they continued their ride, Brooks scanned the grounds, looking for signs of Ruby. She hadn't joined them for breakfast, which was a disappointment. He'd been looking forward to seeing those big brown eyes and the pretty smile this morning. He knew enough to stay away from her, but he had an uncanny, unholy need to see her again.

Now, as they headed back to the stables, he kept his eyes peeled.

"Ruby's got a date this afternoon," his dad said, practically reading his mind. Was Brooks that obvious about what he'd been searching for? He had no right to feel any emotion, yet the one barreling through his belly at hearing Ruby was on a date was undeniable jealousy. "Or she'd be on the ranch today. I've asked her to show you a little about her horse training program. Looks like it's gonna have to wait until tomorrow, if that's okay with you, son?"

"Of course. I'm on Ruby's schedule. She's not on mine. If she's seeing someone, that takes precedence." Damn, if those words weren't hard to force out.

His dad chuckled. "No, it's not like that. Gosh, I'm sure glad that ship has sailed."

"What do you mean?"

"Oh, the man she was seeing a while back didn't sit straight with me. I'm glad he's out of the picture now."

"Didn't like him much, huh?" Brooks shouldn't have been prying, but he couldn't help but want to know more. Ruby fascinated him in every way.

"No. Trace Evans wasn't the man for her. Hurt her real bad, too, and she's moved on. She's having lunch with a girlfriend, and you know how that goes. She could be gone for hours. I told her not to worry and to take all the time she needs. Man, it sure is different raising a girl, that's for sure."

Too much relief to be healthy settled in his gut. "I wouldn't know, having two brothers."

"Yeah, I hear ya. When Ruby came into the family, my boys had to clean up their act. Not a one of them ever disrespected her, and that's what I want for her. Whoever takes her heart better damn well treat it with tender care. I owe it to her and her daddy."

The more he was around Beau, the more respect Brooks had for him. He liked that Beau was watching out for Ruby, and again it underscored his need to keep their relationship platonic. If only he could think of Ruby as a half sister.

Instead of the sexy, hot woman who'd heated up his sheets two nights ago.

Five

Ruby bit into a pulled pork slider, and barbeque sauce dripped down her chin. She dabbed at it with her napkin. "Yum, I feel better already."

Serena Bartolomo chuckled as she lifted her slider to her mouth and took a big bite, too. When it came to settling nerves, there wasn't anything better than the Cool Springs Café's food, and the combination of being with Serena and downing pulled pork made Ruby's hysteria from yesterday seem like a thing of the past.

"So, let me get this straight, Rube. You've got two hot guys in your life right now, and that's what's making you crazy? I should be so lucky."

Serena had her own set of issues with the opposite sex; namely, she was looking for the perfect man. Someone kind, strong, honest and funny, *just like her daddy*, and all others need not apply. It was a tall order, and so far, Serena hadn't found the man of her dreams.

"Luck has everything to do with it," Ruby said. "Bad luck. I thought I had it clear in my mind what I wanted. If the right guy comes along, fine. That would make me happy, I guess. But if he doesn't, and I'm certainly not looking, then I'm good with my horses and family. I'm in no hurry to get hurt again."

"Yeah, Trace did a number on you. I can see you not wanting to jump back into that arena."

"But you should've heard him on the phone, Serena. He was really sweet, and he said everything I wanted to hear. How he missed me. How he's been thinking about me night and day."

"Are you buying it?"

"I shouldn't. But he sounded sincere."

"The rodeo season is over. What will you do if he comes knocking on your door?"

Ruby shrugged. It wasn't as if she hadn't asked herself that question a dozen times already. "I don't know. Wait and see. I'm not rushing into anything."

"That's good, hon."

She released a sigh that emptied her lungs. "And then there's Brooks."

"Yeah, tell me about him."

"Smart, confident, handsome. We had that one night together. A crazy impetuous fling, and afterward we parted ways amicably, only the next day he shows up at Look Away as Beau's long lost son. I never thought I'd see him again, and now he's a fixture at the ranch and I've got to pretend nothing's happened between us."

"Is that hard?"

She sipped from her float, the icy soda sliding down her throat as she contemplated her answer. "Well, it's not easy. Especially with the way he looks at me with those dreamy blue eyes. And he's funny, too. We laugh a lot."

"Uh-oh, that's dangerous. A man who can make you laugh—that's the kiss of death." Serena began shaking her head. "Do you think of Trace at all when you're with him?"

"*Dios*, no. I don't think of any other man when I'm with Brooks. He may not know it yet, but he's so much like his father."

"Being like Beau Preston is a good, good thing."

"So true. But Brooks has a sharper edge, I think. He's pulled himself up from humble beginnings, and this whole situation with not knowing who his real father was has hurt him and maybe made him bitter."

"Wow, that's heavy. Did he tell you that?"

Ruby dipped her head sheepishly, hating to admit the truth. "No, I Googled him. I wanted to find out more about him. He's entering the Preston family, and they've had enough heartache in their lives. Is that horrible? I feel like I'm spying on him."

"It's the way of the world, hon. Don't beat yourself up. You were concerned about Beau, right?"

"Yes, that's part of it. Anyway, now you know my dilemma. Brooks is off-limits to me. He's part of Beau's family now, which means he's my family, too. And then there's Trace. I have to admit, hearing from him last night really threw me off balance."

"Ruby, we've been friends a long time. I know how strong you are. You can handle this. You're Ruby Lopez. Anybody who messes with you lives to regret it."

Ruby laughed. "That's my persona, anyway."

"Hey, you're forgetting I've seen you in action. You've got self-defense skills any woman would love to have."

"Yeah, I can toss a man over my shoulder, no problem. But can I evict him from my heart? That's a totally different matter."

Texas breezes ruffled Brooks's shirt on this warmer than usual December day and brought freshness to the morning as he strode down the path toward the lake. He didn't mind the walk; it helped clear his head. Beau, so proud of his operation here, had recommended that Brooks check out Ruby in action. Hell, he'd already seen her in action. She'd downed a big oaf of a man in that saloon. And then he'd been private witness to her other skills in the bedroom. But of course, Beau had meant something entirely different.

"You want to get a better sense of what we do on Look Away, then go see Ruby down at the lake this morning," his father had said. "She's working with a one-year-old named Cider. Beautiful filly."

The truth was, Brooks hadn't laid eyes on Ruby yesterday, and he'd missed her like crazy. It baffled him just how much. Now, with his boots pounding the earth as he headed her way, his hands locked in his pockets Texas-style, a happy tune was playing in his head. He liked it here. He liked the sun and sky and vastness. He liked the howl of a coyote, the smell of hay and earth and, yes, horse dung. It all seemed so natural and beautiful. But mostly, it was Ruby in this setting that he liked the most.

And there she was, about twenty yards up ahead, near a nameless body of water his father simply called the lake, holding a lead rope in one hand and a long leather stick in the other. She wore a tan hat, her long raven locks gathered in a ponytail that spilled down the back of her red blouse. Skin-tight jeans curved around her ass in a way that made him gulp air.

He lodged himself up against a tree, his arms folded, to take in the scene for a few seconds before he made his presence known. How long had it been since he could simply enjoy watching a woman do her job? Probably never.

Ruby was sweet to the horse, though she wasn't a pushover. She spoke in a friendly voice, using the rope and the stick as tools to train the filly. She was patient, a trait he hadn't associated with Ruby, but then, he really didn't know her all that well. The time she took with the horse notched up his respect for her even more.

"Why don't you come away from the tree, Brooks," she called, catching him off guard. He hadn't seen her look his way; he thought her focus was mainly on the horse she was training. "Cider knows you're here, too."

Brooks marched over to her. "I didn't want to disturb you."

"Too late for that," she said quickly, with a blink of her eyes, maybe surprising herself. He got the feeling she wasn't speaking about the training session. "Actually, I'm glad you're here. Beau wants you to see how we train the horses. And I'm just beginning with Cider."

With gloved hands, she gathered the rope into a circle, her tone businesslike and stiff. It had to be this way, but Brooks didn't like it one bit. He knew she was untouchable, but of course the notion made him want her all the more.

"For the record, you disturb me too, Ruby." He didn't give her a wink or a smile. He wasn't flirting or teasing. He meant it.

"Brooks." She sighed, giving him an eyeful of her innermost thoughts by the sag of her shoulders and the look of hopelessness on her face. Then she turned her full attention to the horse, patting Cider's nose and stroking her long golden mane. "We need to be just friends."

She was stating the obvious.

"I can try," he said.

"For Beau."

"Yeah, for Beau."

Because they both knew if they got together and it didn't work out, Beau would be hurt, as well. Brooks didn't want friction in the Preston family. He was the newcomer. He was trying to fit in and become a part of this family. It would do no good to have a repeat of what happened at the C'mon Inn. His father and this family deserved more than that from him.

Brooks's brain was on board. Now if the rest of him would join in, it wouldn't be an issue at all.

That settled, he gave the horse's nose a stroke. Under his palm, the coarse hair tickled a bit, yet it was also smooth as he slid his hand down. "So, what are you doing with her today?"

"Today, we're working on gullies and water." Ruby jumped right in, eager to share her knowledge. "People sometimes think horses know what's expected of them from birth, but nothing is further from the truth. This girl is water-shy, and she doesn't know how to jump over a gully. Both frighten her. So I'm working with her today to make her more comfortable with both of those situations. Here, let me show you." She walked Cider over to a dip in the property, the gully no more than a yard across. "First I'll let her get familiar with the terrain."

Ruby released the lead rope and, using her stick, tapped the horse on the shoulder. "Don't worry, I'm not hurting her. The stick on the withers or neck lets her know she's crowding my space. When she gets scared, she closes in on me. I'm trying to get her into her own space."

Ruby worked the horse up and down the area. The horse avoided the gulley altogether. Ruby gave the horse room to investigate, leading her with the rope. "See that, Brooks? She's stopped to sniff and get her bearings. That's good. Now I'm going to bring her in a little closer. She won't like it much—she doesn't know what to do about the gully—but she'll figure it out. I keep sending her closer and closer to the gap and tapping, like this." She tapped Cider again and then gave the horse time to overcome her fear. Back and forth, back and forth. Then Cider stopped again, put her head down and sniffed around. The next time Ruby led her close to the gulley, she jumped. "There! Good girl. That's wonderful, Cider." She stroked the horse again, giving praise. "Good girl. Want to try it one more time?

"I'll keep this going," Ruby explained to him. "Leading her back and forth near the gully. And soon she'll be a pro at jumping over it. It's a start."

"It's amazing how she responds to you, Ruby. I saw a change in her in just a few minutes. Will she go in the water?"

"She'll go near it and take a drink. But she won't go into the water. That takes a bit more time. She's thirsty now, which will work in my favor. But I won't push her right now. She can have a peaceful drink."

Ruby let the rope hang very loose, taking off any

pressure, and approached the water. Cider resisted for a few seconds. Then, without being prompted by the stick or the rope, she walked over to the bank and dipped her head to lap up water. "See how wary she is? She won't put her feet in. But she will, very soon."

"I never thought about horses not feeling inherently comfortable with their surroundings. I don't know a whole lot about horses, that's for damn sure. I guess I figured they were naturally at ease with jumping and going in the water."

"Yeah, I know that's the perception. But horses, like children, need to be trained to do the things we know they are capable of doing. They certainly don't under-stand what it means when we put saddles on them or bits in their mouths. The truth is, when I train the horses, they tell me what they need help with. And I listen and watch. The reason this method works so well is that I give the horse a purpose. I kept sending Cider across that gully and let her figure out how to solve the prob-lem. It's a matter of knowing what they need and pro-viding it."

Brooks spent the remainder of the morning watch-ing Ruby work miracles with this horse, completely im-pressed with her knowledge and the ease with which she worked. When his stomach grumbled, he grinned. "Are you going back to the house for lunch?"

"No. I'm not done with Cider yet. I brought my lunch out here."

"You're eating here?"

"Yep, under that tree you were holding up earlier."

He laughed. "Sounds peaceful."

She stared into his eyes. "It is."

"Okay, then, I should get going. Let you have your lunch."

He turned and began walking.

"There's enough for two," she said, a hitch in her throat, as if she couldn't believe she'd just said that. Hell, if she was inviting, he wouldn't be refusing.

He turned and smiled. "If it's Lupe's leftover fried chicken, I'm taking you up on it."

"And what if it isn't?" she asked.

"I'm still staying."

Ruby's mouth pulled into a frown as if she was having second thoughts.

"As your friend," he added.

Her tight expression relaxed, and a glint gleamed in her pretty brown eyes. "I lied. It is chicken, and Lupe packed me way too much."

"So then, I'd be doing you a favor by staying and eating with you. Wouldn't want all that food to go to waste."

She rolled her eyes adorably, and Brooks was glad to see the Ruby of old come back.

She grabbed her backpack, and together they walked over to the tree where swaying branches provided shade on the packed-dirt ground. Ruby tossed her stuff down, but before she sat, he put up his hand. "Wait a sec."

She stood still, her eyes sharp as he pulled his shirt

out of his jeans and began unbuttoning until his white T-shirt was exposed. "Never did like this shirt anyway." He took off his shirt and made a bit of a production laying it on the ground. Then he gestured to Ruby. "Now you can sit."

Her expression warmed considerably. "Galahad. You're too much."

"That's what they tell me."

She plopped herself comfortably down on his shirt so that her perfect behind wouldn't be ground into the dirt. "Thank you. You know, that's about the sweetest thing a man's done for me in a long while."

"Well then, you're meeting the wrong kind of men. Present company excluded. And boy, am I glad you're not into all that feminism stuff, or I'd be dead meat right now."

She smiled. "Who says I'm not? I believe in the power of women."

"So do I."

"But I can also recognize a gentleman when I see one, and I don't feel like it's diminishing my role in the world."

"And this is Texas, after all," he said.

"Right."

"And I have developed Southern charm."

"Don't press your luck, Preston."

Brooks blinked. And then he looked straight into Ruby's spirited chocolate eyes. "Thanks. It feels good to be called by my father's name."

"You're welcome. You've earned it."

He stared at her and nodded, holding back a brand-new emotion welling behind his eyes.

Brooks headed to the main house that evening, thoughts of Ruby never far from his mind. The more time he spent with her… Okay, forget it. He couldn't go down that road, especially when the main reason his thoughts had splintered was standing not ten feet away on the sweeping porch of the residence.

As soon as Beau spotted Brooks, he called him over with a wave of the hand. "Come here, son. Meet the rest of the family."

The three men—all wearing Stetsons in varying colors and appearing younger than Brooks by several years—stood at attention next to Beau. Brooks's half brothers.

He walked up, and Beau gave his shoulder a squeeze. "Brooks, I'm proud to introduce you to Toby, Clay and Malcolm. They're your brothers."

He shook each one of their hands and greeted them kindly. It was strange and awkward at first, but Beau's boys made him feel welcome.

"We're surely glad to meet you," Toby said. He was the oldest and tallest of the three. "I'm sorry we missed out on knowing you all those years."

"Yeah, I'm sorry, too. Life took me down a different path," he said.

Malcolm stood against the post, his boots crossed,

his gaze narrowing in on Brooks's face. "But you're here now, and we're glad of it. You look more like Dad than any of us."

Beau chuckled. "Poor guy."

"Mom wouldn't agree," Clay said, chiming in. "She was always telling us how handsome you were."

"Yeah," Malcolm said. "Damn near gave us a complex."

Beau shook his head. "Your mama thought the sun rose and set on you boys, and you know it."

"Seems like your mom was a pretty great lady from what I'm told," Brooks said. He'd heard from Beau, but just about everyone else on the ranch had nice things to say about Tanya, too.

"That she was," Beau said, the pride in his voice unequalled.

"My brothers and I, well, we're sorry to hear news of your mother's passing, Brooks," Malcolm said. The others nodded in agreement.

"Thank you. Mom was also quite a woman. And she died unexpectedly. My brothers and I miss her terribly."

"It's not easy," Beau said, the brightness in his eyes dimming. "But we have each other now, and that's something to celebrate. Shall we go in to dinner? Lupe promised us a feast, and we're opening a few special bottles of wine to toast the occasion."

"I'm nearly starved," Toby said, patting his stomach.

"Yeah, me, too," Clay said. "Oh, and new brother?"

Brooks gave him a glance. "Yeah?"

"I'm apologizing in advance for the interrogation. We're all so dang curious about your life, I'm afraid we're gonna grill you. We want to hear about Graham, too. Dad says he's the spitting image of you."

"Yep, there are two of us. We're identical twins."

"You boys will meet him soon," Beau said as he ushered them all into the house. "I'm hoping Graham will be here by next week in time for our Christmas party."

"I don't mind your questions," Brooks added. "I've got quite a few for you. We all have some catching up to do."

In the formal dining room, on Beau's cue, Clay, Malcolm and Toby spent the next few minutes asking about Brooks's early life, his college days and how he came to build such a successful real estate development business. "Lots of hard work, long hours and a driving need to make my way in the world," he answered. "Mom was a survivor, and she raised her children to be independent thinkers."

Beau smiled, getting a faraway look in his eyes. Was he thinking about the young woman he'd loved and lost? Then, with a shake of the head, he shifted and turned his attention back to the conversation.

Lupe came in, carrying plates filled with twelve-ounce rib eye steaks, potatoes, creamed corn and Texas-sized biscuits. "Looks delicious, Lupe. Thank you," Beau said.

Toby and Malcolm immediately rose to help her bring the rest of the food in from the kitchen. And just as they were sitting down, ready to take their first bite, Ruby walked in.

She didn't immediately make eye contact with Brooks, so he looked his fill. Her jeans and blousy top were white, but her ankle boots were as black as the mass of long raven hair falling down her back. The contrast of black to white was striking, and he took a swallow of water to keep his mouth from going dry. "Hey, everyone," she said.

"Better late than never, Rube," Clay said, teasing. "Had another hot date with a horse?"

Toby and Malcolm chuckled.

"Wouldn't you like to know," she said, smiling and scooting her fine little ass into her seat. "At least horses can take direction. Unlike most men I know."

Beau choked out a laugh.

Ruby arched a brow and shot daggers at Clay. Apparently she wasn't through with him yet. "And tell me again, who are you dating at the moment?"

"Oh, you've dug yourself a hole now, Clay," Malcolm said. "You know better than to get into it with Ruby. You're not gonna win."

"You see," she said, "Malcolm understands. At least he has a girlfriend."

"This is a picture of what it was like when the kids were growing up," Beau explained, grinning. "I gotta say, it's still amusing."

Ruby glanced at Brooks then, giving him a nod of acknowledgment. He smiled, acknowledging how Ruby held her own with Beau's boys. She was a handful, a woman with spunk who took no prisoners and didn't apologize for it. If only he could stop noticing all her admirable traits. As it was now, she was off the charts.

Wine was poured and Beau lifted his glass. Everyone at the table took his cue, and the deep red wine in the raised glasses glistened under chandelier light. "To my family," he said. "I couldn't be happier to have Brooks here. And soon Graham will join us. I love you all," he said, his voice tight, "and look forward to the day we can all be together."

Glasses clinked and Brooks was touched at the welcome he'd received by his new family at Look Away Ranch.

They settled into the meal. The steak was the most tender he'd ever had. Texans knew a thing or two about raising prime cattle and delivering a delicious meal. His brothers surely looked the picture of health—all three were sturdy men—and a sense of pride in his newfound family washed over him. He doubted he'd ever feel as close to these young men as he did Graham—he and Graham had shared too much together—but he hoped they'd all become the family Beau had longed for.

"Dad says our little sis taught you a thing or two about horse training," Toby remarked. "What'd you think?"

Brooks hesitated a second, finishing a sip of wine while contemplating how to answer the innocent question. He couldn't give too much away. He couldn't say that Ruby was the most amazing woman he'd ever met, or that her talent and skill and patience had inspired him. That would be too telling, wouldn't it? "What I know about horses, I'm afraid to say, can fit in this wineglass. But watching Ruby at work and hearing her thoughts on training gave me a whole new perspective. It's eye-opening. It seems Ruby has just the right touch."

Toby nodded. "She does. We've all had a hand in horse training growing up, and all of our techniques are different, but the honest truth is, when we'd come up against a stubborn one that gave us trouble, we turned to Ruby and she'd find a way. Now she pretty much runs the show."

Brooks looked at Ruby, giving her a smile. "I see that she pretty much runs the show around here, too."

Beau chuckled. "Didn't take you long to figure that out."

"There's an advantage to being the only female in the family," Malcolm said.

"I can speak for myself, Mal," she chimed in. "There's an advantage to being the only female in the family."

Everyone laughed.

Ruby's eyes twinkled, and in that moment, Brooks felt like one of them. A Preston, through and through.

The next morning, Beau suggested that they spend the day with Ruby. There was more she could teach

Brooks, and if he really wanted to get a sense of how the operation was run, he needed to get his hands dirty.

"Ruby will put you in touch with your inner wrangler," Beau joked.

Well, she'd already put him in touch with *something*: namely, rock-solid lust. The woman turned him inside out, and there was no help for it.

Before Brooks had even met Ruby, he'd asked for this training, and Beau was more than happy to accommodate his request. But now it meant that Brooks and Ruby would get to spend more time together at the Look Away. Yet Brooks wanted to learn. He needed to catch up on the history of the ranch and the day-to-day operation of running it. It would give him a chance to meet Beau and his half brothers on equal ground. He'd have more in common with each one of them if he could grasp at least a basic knowledge of horses, training and all that went with them.

So they'd walked over to one of the corrals and stood by the fence, watching Ruby securing a saddle on an unruly stallion.

The air was brisk this morning, the sun shadowed by gray clouds. He huddled up in his own wool-lined jacket and noted that Ruby, too, was dressed in a dark quilted vest over a flannel shirt. Only Ruby Lopez could make regular cowgirl gear look sexy. "Morning," she said, greeting both of them.

"Morning," he replied. But she had already turned

away, busy with the horse, restraining his jerky movements with a firm hand on his bridle.

"This is Spirit," Beau said. "He's got a lot to learn, doesn't he, Ruby?"

"He sure does. He's not taken kindly to wearing a saddle. He's going to hate it even more once I ride him. But that's not happening today."

The horse snorted and shuffled his feet, pulling back and away from her. "Hold steady, boy," Ruby said, her voice smooth as fine silk. "You're not gonna like any of this, are you now?"

The horse bucked, and Brooks made a move to lunge over the fence to help Ruby. Beau restrained him with a hand to the chest. "Hang on. Ruby's a pro. She won't put herself in danger."

Brooks wasn't too sure about that. The tall stallion dwarfed Ruby in size and weight. Watching her outmaneuver the animal made Brooks's heart stop for a moment. Hell, she could be crushed. She slid him a sideways glance, her beautiful eyes telling him she'd just seen what he'd done. What was it she called him? Galahad. Hell, he was no knight in shining armor. To most of the people who knew him in Chicago, that label would be laughable. But today, right in this moment, he didn't give a crap about what anyone called him. But he did care about Ruby, and it surprised him how much. He didn't want to see her get trampled. "Are you sure? That horse looks dangerous."

"He could be, but Ruby knows her limitations. She's

got a way about her that outranks his stature. She's gaining his trust right now. Though it doesn't look like it, she's giving him some leeway to put up a fuss. This is his second day wearing a saddle. He's got to get used to it, is all."

"It takes a lot of patience, I see."

"Yep," Beau said. "For the trainer and the animal."

For the next hour, Brooks watched Ruby put the horse through his paces. Every now and then, she'd inform him what she was doing and how the horse should respond. Nine times out of ten, the horse didn't make a liar out of her.

Beau had excused himself a short time ago. He had a meeting with his accountant, and though he invited Brooks to join in, he'd also warned that it would bore him out of his wits. Brooks had opted to stay and watch Ruby work with the stallion. He could watch that woman for hours without being bored, but he didn't tell his father that.

When Ruby was done, she unsaddled Spirit carefully, speaking to the horse lovingly and stroking him softly on the withers. Then she set him free, and he took off running along the perimeter of the large oval corral, his charcoal mane flying in the breeze.

Ruby closed the gate behind her and walked over to Brooks, removing her leather gloves and pocketing them.

"Impressive," he said.

"Thanks. Spirit will come around. He's a Thorough-bred, and they tend to be high-strung."

"Is that so?" Brooks met her gaze. "Sort of reminds me of someone I know."

Her index finger pressed into her chest. "Me?"

"Yeah, you." Her finger rested in the hollow between her breasts. If only he didn't remember how damn intoxicating it'd been when he'd touched her there. How soft she'd felt, how incredibly beautiful and full her breasts were. The thought of never touching Ruby like that again grated on him.

"Well, you're half-right," she said. "Both my parents were Mexican, so I'm a purebred."

"What about the other half?"

"I'm not high-strung or high-maintenance. I'm strong-willed, determined. Some have called me feisty."

"And they lived to tell about it?"

She snapped her head up and saw his grin. "You're teasing me, Galahad."

What he was doing was flirting. He couldn't help it. Ruby, being Ruby, was an aphrodisiac he couldn't combat. And he was beginning to like her nickname for him. "Yeah, I am."

She smiled back for a second, her eyes latching onto his. Then his gaze dropped to her perfectly sweet mouth. Suddenly all the things he'd done to that mouth came crashing into his mind. And all the things she'd done to him with that mouth…

"Spirit," she said, "uh, he'll bring in a good sum."

She began walking. And now she was back to business and a much safer subject. It was necessary, but Brooks had to say he was disappointed. He walked beside her as they headed into the stable.

"He will?"

"Absolutely, once we find the right buyer."

He squinted to adjust to the darkness inside the furthest reaches of the barn. It was even colder in here than outside.

Ruby grabbed a bucket, a brush and a shoe pick. "Beau's been great about giving me input on who our horses end up with. Especially the stallions. They're in demand, but not everyone is cut out to own one."

"You mean you can tell when someone is all wrong for the horse?"

She handed him the brush and a bucket.

"Pretty much."

"That's a talent I never knew existed."

"It's no different than anything else. You wouldn't buy a car you didn't feel was the right fit. A mom of three wouldn't do too well in a sports car. The same holds true for a single guy on the dating scene. He isn't going to buy a dependable sedan to impress a girl, now is he?"

Brooks smiled. "I never thought of it that way."

"The horses I train need to go to good homes. They need to fit. Spirit wouldn't do well with a young boy, for instance. He's not going to be someone's first horse. But a seasoned rider, someone who knows animals, will be able to handle him, no problem. Beau has built his business on putting his horses with the right owners. It's a partnership."

Ruby removed her hat and stuck it on a knob on the wall. With a flick of the wrist, she unleashed her mane of dark hair, and it tumbled down her back. It was the little uncensored, unknowing moves that made Ruby so damn appealing. She was pretty without trying and as free a spirit as the horse she'd just trained.

"What?" she asked, catching Brooks staring.

"Nothing." He stepped closer. "No, that's not true," he said. "I'm standing here, looking at you and wondering how the hell I'm going to keep from touching you again."

She got a look in her eyes, one he couldn't read, and bit down on her lip. "We, uh, w-we can't."

But it was what she said with her eyes, and her stutter when she denied him, that gave him hope. "It's hard for you, too. You like me."

"I like a lot of things. But I love Beau. And I don't want to—"

"Ruby." The bucket and brush fell from Brooks's hands and thumped to the ground. She gasped as he approached. He took hold of her arms gently, and her chin tipped up. He gazed into defiant eyes. Was she telling him to back off or daring him to kiss her? There was only one way to find out. "Ruby," he rasped and walked her backward against the wall. There was no way anyone could glimpse them from outside. They were alone but for dozens of horses. "You want this, too," he whispered, and then his mouth touched hers, and the sweetest purr escaped her throat. He deepened the kiss, tasting her again, her warmth, the softness of her lips burning through him.

She threaded her arms around his neck, tugging him forward, making him hot all over. She was a dynamo, a fiery woman who kissed him back with enough passion to set the darn barn on fire. Their bodies melded together, a perfect fit of small to large. They'd made it work one time before, and it had been heaven on earth. He wanted that again. He wanted to touch her and make her cry out. He wanted to strip her naked and watch her body move under his.

One kiss from Ruby had him forgetting all else. It was crazy. It was the middle of the day and they were in his father's stable. But none of that mattered right now. Brooks couldn't stop. He couldn't walk away from Ruby. He grabbed thick locks of her hair, the shiny mass silky in his hands. He gave a tug and gazed down at her, so beautiful, so full of passion. "Is there somewhere we can go?" His voice was rough, needy.

Her eyes closed for a second as she decided, the pause making his heart stop. But then she whispered, "My office behind the tack room. There's a lock."

Relieved, he gave a slight nod of his head and then gripping her bottom, lifted her. Her legs wrapped around his waist, and he carried her to the office. He maneuvered them inside, turned the lock and then lowered her down. As soon as her feet hit the ground, she moved to the window and twisted the lever to close the blinds.

It gave him a second to do a cursory survey of her office. Warm tones, a wood floor, a cluttered desk and a dark leather sofa were all he needed to know about the decor before he turned to Ruby again, taking her back into his arms and claiming her mouth.

It wasn't long before their desperate whimpers and growls filled the room. He stripped Ruby of her vest pretty quickly and then worked the buttons of her blouse. She helped, and then he pushed the layers off her shoulders and undid her lacy black bra. Her breasts spilled out, and he simply looked at her in awe for a few seconds before filling his hands. He flicked his thumbs over both nipples. She sucked in oxygen and squeezed her eyes closed, the pleasure on her face adding fuel to his fire.

As he bent his head and drew her nipple into his mouth, she moaned low and painfully deep. Her hands were in his hair, holding him there, as if he needed the extra encouragement.

"Galahad," she whispered softly.

"Hmm?"

"Get naked."

She was impatient, and maybe he was, too, because if he stopped to analyze this, to really think about what was happening and *where*, rational thoughts would intrude and possibly kill the moment. He couldn't have that. He was too far gone, and so was Ruby. He could tell by the sounds she was making and the desperate look in her eyes.

This was dangerous in so many ways, and yet neither of them could put a halt to what they were doing, so he quickly unfastened all the buttons on his shirt.

And then Ruby's hands were on him, pulling his shirt off and tossing it aside. Her fingertips began grazing his skin, probing his chest as she planted kisses here and there. She reached for the waistband of his jeans and pulled his zipper down. "You're right," he murmured. "You are feisty."

"Determined," she corrected him, and he actually chuckled through the flames burning him to the quick.

"Your turn," he said, dipping into the waistband of her jeans. Within seconds, he had her naked and trembling. He couldn't blame her; he was equally turned on. All the secrecy and danger might have added to it, but it could simply have been Ruby. She was a man's dream. Maybe she could've been *his* dream in a different life.

She was feathery light in his arms as he lifted her and carried her to the sofa. He laid her down and gazed at her for a moment. Her hair, her skin, her body, everything that was Ruby made him shiver and want to please her. He came down next to her, squeezing in beside her on the sofa. He kissed her hard then, crushing his mouth to hers while moving his hand to her sweet spot. She bucked as he began to caress her. "Enjoy this, Ruby. Don't hold back. You understand?"

She nodded eagerly.

And he worked up a sweat pleasing her, using his kisses to muffle her whimpers and moans. And when her final jolt released her ultimate pleasure, he was there with her to press his mouth to hers and swallow her soft cries.

It was a heady thing, satisfying Ruby, but they weren't through yet. He rose up immediately, and she helped him take off the rest of his clothes. He grabbed for the packet he carried in his pocket and sheathed himself before coming up over Ruby. She stretched her arms up, reaching around his neck to pull him down and kiss him again. He was ready, so ready, and when Ruby invited him into her warmth, he joined them together in one breathtaking plunge.

Aw, hell. It was better than he remembered. He stilled, absorbing the feel of her, loving the body that so readily welcomed him.

"Don't hold back, Galahad. You understand?"

Good God, Ruby was something. He kissed her again and again, and as he moved deeper, filling her body, she moved with him, keeping pace, rising and lifting and enjoying.

It happened swiftly, neither one wanting to wait, both desperate to find that place that would unite them on the highest ground. She called out his name, and quickly he muted her with a powerful kiss. Then her hips bowed up, and he propelled her even higher with one final all-consuming push. The rush made her convulse around him, and he couldn't hold back any longer. He came as close to heaven as any mortal man could.

Afterward he lay holding Ruby in his arms. "You all right?"

She nodded, unable to speak.

He kissed her forehead, stroking her arm and grazing his fingers over the peaks of her lush breasts. Then he slid his hand down to her legs. He caressed her there, taking in the smooth, soft skin under his palms, not knowing when he'd have the privilege of doing this again.

He heard the thud of footsteps coming toward the office. Voices filtered in.

Ruby's eyes rounded, and she gasped. "It's Sam and one of the boys," she whispered. "He may be looking for me. I left Spirit in the corral, and the grooming equipment is all over the ground. Damn it."

"Shh. Don't panic. I locked the door."

"But Sam knows I never lock the door when I'm working. If he knocks on the door, I won't be able to look him in the eye. Not with you in here. I've got to go."

She rose and donned her clothes hastily, then wove her fingers through her hair to tame the messy locks. "Get dressed, Brooks. And don't come out of the office until I get them out of here."

"Ruby, it wouldn't be the end of the world if they saw me in your office."

"Are you insane? I'd never be able to pull that off.

Sam will know something's up and it's the last thing either of us need right now. Stay until it's safe for you to leave."

She opened the door and was gone.

Leaving him locked in the office, buck naked.

What the hell?

Six

Ruby sat down in front of her flat-screen TV and began eating cold chicken salad. She'd deliberately not gone to dinner at the main house tonight. How could she possibly have faced Brooks across the table, eaten a meal with her family and pretended there was nothing between her and Brooks? She was still at odds with herself for what had happened in her office this afternoon. They'd come very close to being discovered. Sneaking around wasn't in her DNA. She didn't like subterfuge.

But wow. And double wow. When it came to Brooks, she didn't seem to have much resistance. Just a look, a word from him, tied her into knots. She had trouble fending him off and found that most times, she didn't want to. She enjoyed his company a little too much.

A nighttime soap opera played on the screen, a story about oil and country music and cowboys who were too much trouble. She stared at the TV as she forked lettuce into her mouth, trying to concentrate on the story and not the city dude with the deep sky-blue eyes who had turned her simple ranch life upside down lately.

A familiar voice sounded and she blinked. Trace Evans walked into the picture and her spine straightened as she sat up and took notice. Trace was on television?

He had a bit part; he spoke a few words before he disappeared again.

Now, this was news. Trace hadn't told her anything about it. But then, she hadn't spoken with him in ages, except for that one phone call a few days ago. Funny that he didn't mention anything about being on *Homestead Hills*, even if it was only a small role. She continued to watch, finishing her salad and waiting for him to appear again.

He didn't.

A knock at her door made her jump. She clicked off the TV and rose from the sofa. Her mind still on Trace, she walked to the door and looked through the peephole. It was Brooks. Seeing him on her doorstep caused her belly to stir immediately. He always made her forget all about Trace and the heartache he'd put her through.

She opened the door and stared into smiling, deep blue eyes. He held a bunch of flowers in one hand and a lavender box from Cool Springs Confections in the other. "Hello, Ruby."

"Brooks, come inside." She ushered him in before someone spotted him with date night goodies in his arms. She scanned her yard before closing the door, thankful that no one was in sight. She had no business being alone with Brooks, but she wasn't about to throw him out, either.

He stood just inside her cottage and grinned. "You look uptight, Ruby."

If it wasn't for the light in his eyes, she might have been offended. "Thanks to you. You really shouldn't be here."

"I do a lot of things I shouldn't do. These are for you." He handed her a dozen beautiful white roses and the box of chocolates. "Listen, I'm not courting you. Well, not in the usual sense."

"Not in any sense," she pointed out.

"Still, we've been thrown together and it's been… amazing." He pushed his hand through his blond hair as he struggled for words. "I don't know. I had to come. To give you something nice, something you deserve. The way you had to run out from the office after we made love didn't sit well with me."

"Thank you, Brooks. But you don't owe me anything. As you said, we're not dating. We never could be, and I did what was necessary."

"I've learned never to say never, Ruby." He glanced at her arms loaded with his gifts. "You want to put those flowers in water?"

"Uh, sure. Follow me," she said, leading him into the

kitchen. She set the box of candy on the table and then opened a cupboard door. "They really are gorgeous."

"I'm glad you like them."

"I don't remember seeing such perfect white roses this time of year in Cool Springs."

"They're not from Cool Springs. I had them flown in from Chicago."

She craned her head around. "You didn't."

He shrugged and gave her a simple nod. Her heart beat a little bit harder.

"My florist is known for his perfect roses. Cool Springs didn't have anything that comes close."

She kept forgetting he was a zillionaire. He probably did this kind of thing all the time for the women in his life. Though that might be true, the sweet gesture and the trouble he'd gone through weren't lost on her. "It's nice of you, Brooks."

She found a crystal vase, an heirloom from her grandmother, and filled it with water. Arranging the flowers, she placed the vase in the center of her glass-top kitchen table. "Here we go."

"It's a nice place you have here," Brooks said.

"It was my father's house, and I've sort of made it my own."

Once Ruby was old enough to make changes, she had redecorated the place, adding modern furniture and window treatments that aligned more with who she was. The cottage wasn't rustic anymore but had a bit of style and flair. She enjoyed living here when she wasn't at her apartment in town.

"I can see your personality here," Brooks said.

Why did he always know the right thing to say?

"Then I've succeeded. It was a labor of love decorating the cottage."

Brooks looked down at the box of candy on the table. "I hear Cool Springs Confections makes a pretty good chocolate buttercream candy."

"That's what they're known for. Want to try one? I can make coffee, or—"

"Sure, I'll try one. And coffee would be great."

"Have a seat. I'll get the coffee going."

"Can I do anything?"

"Grab two mugs from the cupboard above the stove."

"Sure thing."

A few minutes later, she poured two cups of coffee and sat down with Brooks at her kitchen table, realizing this could be dangerous. Spending time with Brooks always seemed to be, yet he was easy company and someone she truly liked. She opened the box and glanced at a dozen luscious candies. "It's going to be hard to choose. Here's a buttercream for you." She pointed it out and he grabbed it.

"I think I'll try the raspberry chocolate," she said.

"Is that your favorite?" he asked.

"It is." She didn't wait for Brooks. She took a big bite and let the soft, creamy raspberry center ooze down her throat. "Oh, yum."

Brooks grinned and then downed his candy in one giant swallow. "Wow, that was good."

"Have another," she said. "I'm going to."

They sipped coffee between bites and managed to polish off half the box of chocolates. Brooks took a last swallow of coffee and then set down his mug. "We're not going to talk about what happened in the stable?"

She replaced the lid on the box, stalling for time, and then finally replied, "No. I don't think so."

"So we just pretend there isn't this *thing* between us."

"We don't have to pretend anything."

"All right," he said, rising and reaching for her hand. "No more pretending we're not hot for each other, Ruby. The truth is, I can't stop thinking about you." He gave her hand a tug, lifting her from her seat. He was deadly handsome, but more than that, he wasn't playing games with her the way Trace had. With Brooks she felt special and cared for, and maybe he was what she needed to get over Trace. She'd protected her heart and would continue to do so, but she had Brooks on the brain lately. She knew he would eventually go back to Chicago. He belonged in the city, and her place was here. Maybe they could keep things light. "I came here only to give you the flowers, Ruby," he said. "I had no ulterior motive."

"Really? I thought you needed a good reason to down half a box of candy."

"That, too." But the truth was in his eyes, and her heart did that thing it did when she was with him. It spun out of control.

She lifted herself on tiptoe and placed a soft kiss on his lips. "You're sweet."

He growled from deep in his throat, a desperate sound that resembled exactly how she was feeling right now, and then his gaze fell to her mouth. His eyes darkening, he backed up a step and put some distance between them. "It really was about the flowers, Ruby. I'd better go." He turned and headed toward the door.

Seeing him retreat put thoughts of the lonely night ahead in her mind. "You don't have to go," she blurted the second he reached for the doorknob. "I mean…you don't have to rush off. I was just going to pop a movie in and kick back. If you care to join me, I have popcorn."

"That was the deal breaker," he said, his lips twitching. "'Cause if you didn't have popcorn, I was out the door."

"Go sit in the living room, Galahad. I'll be right in."

"Thanks—and oh, I like lots of butter."

She rolled her eyes, and he laughed. "Anything else?"

"No, just you and the popcorn make it a perfect night."

Ruby hummed her way into the kitchen and grinned the whole time the kernels were popping.

Ruby sat cross-legged on the sofa next to Brooks, the fireplace giving heat and a warm glow to the room. They'd emptied the popcorn bowl a long while ago, and the movie was ending, but she wasn't ready for him to leave. She was nestled comfortably in the crook of his shoulder, and neither one of them made a move to separate when the credits rolled. There was a sense of rightness when they were together, which should have scared her off. She wasn't looking to get her heart broken again. But it was harder to see him leave than it was to have him here. She didn't know what to make of that.

"That was good," she said of the classic Western they'd just watched. "I've seen it half a dozen times, and it never disappoints." What wasn't to like about horses and range wars and white hats against black hats? It was clear who to cheer for, who were the good guys. If only life was that easy to figure out.

Her body had been in a constant state of high alert since Brooks entered the house. She'd tried hard to tamp down her feelings, to treat him as a guest and not the man who'd turned her inside out. A part of her wanted him to go, so that they could end whatever they had before he tore her life up in shreds. And another part of her wanted him to stay. To keep her company throughout the cold winter night.

She lifted away from Brooks and unfolded her pretzel position to stretch out her legs.

He planted his feet on the floor, bracing his elbows on his knees, and turned to her. "Thanks for the movie. I really liked it. But I think a lot of that had to do with the company."

She smiled. "Thank you."

"Welcome. Popcorn was good, too. I can't remember enjoying an evening like this back home."

"You don't go to movies in Chicago?"

He shook his head. "No, not really. I'm usually too busy. It's not high on my list of priorities."

"I guess Cool Springs is a totally different experience from what you're used to."

"It is, but not in a bad way. Back home, my phone is ringing constantly. My life is full of dinner meetings and weekends of work. I don't get to play very often."

"Is that what you're doing here? Playing?"

"If you knew how hard I tried to find Beau, you wouldn't even have to ask. I went to great lengths and sometimes, now that I think back, didn't employ the most honorable means to locate my father. My coming to Look Away is very serious. But I am finding some peace here, and it's quite surprising."

"I meant with me, Brooks."

He reached out to grab her hand, then turned it over in his palm as he contemplated her question. "Not with you, either, Ruby. I don't make a habit of playing games, period."

"You probably don't have to."

"Meaning?"

"Meaning, you're handsome and wealthy and I bet—"

"You'd bet wrong. I'd be the first one to tell you I've been obsessed lately with finding the truth of my parentage. I haven't had a moment for anything else. I haven't dated in months, and I—"

She pressed her fingers against his lips. "Okay, I believe you."

He kissed her fingertips. "Good." He rose then and lifted her to her feet on his way up. "I really should go."

She waited a beat, debating over whether to have him in her bed tonight, to wake with him in the morning. Picturing it was like a dream, but she couldn't do it. She couldn't invite him to stay. The long list of reasons why not infiltrated her mind, making it all very clear.

"I'll walk you out." She tugged on his hand and headed to the door, ignoring the regret in his eyes and willing away her own doubts about letting him go. "Thanks for the candy and flowers, Brooks."

He bent his head and kissed her lightly on the lips. The kiss was over before she knew what was happening. "You're welcome. I had a nice time tonight," he said and walked out the door.

He had had no ulterior motive for showing up here tonight.

Her heart warmed at the thought.

Galahad had been true to his word.

The next morning, Ruby entered the shed attached to the main house. It was nearly as big as the Preston five-car garage. Back in the day, the Preston boys would play in here, pretending to camp out in the dark walled recesses and holding secret meetings. Ruby was never a part of that all-boy thing, but she had her own secrets in this place. The shed was where twelve-year-old Rusty

Jenkins had given her her first kiss. It had been an amateur attempt, she realized years later, as the boy's lips were as soft as a baby's and he'd kinda slobbered. But it had thrilled her since Rusty was a boy she'd really liked. And every time she walked in here, those old, very sweet memories flooded her mind.

She lifted the first box she found marked Christmas in red lettering and loaded it into her arms. Ever since Tanya had passed on, Beau enlisted Ruby's help in decorating the entire house, claiming the place needed a woman's touch. And she was happy to do it. It was serious business getting the house ready for the holidays.

When the shed door opened, letting in cool Texas air, she called, "Beau, I'm back here."

"We're coming," Beau said in a nasal voice.

She turned to find not one but two Prestons approaching. She should've known Brooks would be with him. There was no help for it; Beau was anxious to spend as much time as he could with his son.

Immediately Beau took the box out of her arms. "Morning, Ruby."

"Good morning," she said to both of them. But her gaze lingered on Brooks, dressed in faded blue jeans and a white T-shirt that hugged his biceps. She looked away instantly—she couldn't let Beau catch her drooling over his son. Brooks had *hunk* written all over him, and how well she knew. Every time he entered a room, her blood pulsed wildly. It usually took a few moments to calm down. "Brooks is going to help us decorate the tree, if that's okay with you." Beau barely got the words out before he began coughing, and his face turned candy apple red.

"Are you sick, Beau?" she asked.

"Trying to catch a cold is all, Rube."

But he coughed again and again. Brooks grabbed the box out of his arms.

"Not trying," she said. "You sound terrible. You're congested, Beau."

"I think so, too, but he insisted on helping decorate the tree today," Brooks said.

Beau pursed his lips. It was the closest the man came to pouting. "Is it so wrong to want to put up a tree with my son for the first time?"

Ruby glanced at Brooks and then gave Beau a sweet smile. "Not at all, but if you're not feeling well, you should rest. The Look Away Christmas party is happening this weekend, and Graham and his fiancée will be here by then. You want to be healthy for that, Beau. A little rest will do you a world of good. I can manage the tree."

"I'll help, Ruby," Brooks added, nodding. "Why not take a rest and come down later for dinner?"

Beau turned his head away and coughed a blue streak. "Okay," he managed on a nod. He couldn't argue after that coughing spell. "I guess you two are right. I can't be sick when Graham and Eve get here. Not with her being pregnant and all. That's my first grandbaby." Pride filled his voice.

"Yeah, and I'm gonna be an uncle." Brooks's eyes gleamed, showing Ruby just how much Beau and Brooks looked alike.

"That you are." Then Beau drew out a sigh as if he wanted to do anything but rest on his laurels this morning. "I'll go now. See you both later on."

He walked away, and the sound of his coughing followed him out the door.

Now Ruby was alone in the shed with deadly handsome Brooks. He stared at her, a smile on his face.

"What?" she asked.

"You're a bossy mother hen."

She shook her head. "I already lost one father. Don't want to lose another."

Brooks flinched, and she wished she could take her words back. Brooks hadn't meant anything by his comment. He was teasing; it was what he did, and she shouldn't have lashed out. But the man made her a little jumpy and whole lot of crazy.

"I'm sorry. It's just that my father worked himself into the ground, and I was too young to know enough to stop him. Losing him as a teen was hard. I had no other family, and when Beau took me in and treated me as his own, well…it meant a lot to me. So I'm protective."

Brooks moved a stray hair from her cheek and tucked it back behind her ear. "I get that. I was only teasing."

"I know." She lifted her chin and cracked a small smile.

"Ruby," he said quietly. His eyes softened to a blue

glow, his hand moving to the back of her neck to hold her head in place.

There was silent communication between them. She sensed that he understood, and in the silence of the shed, her heart pounded as she stared at him, wishing that he was someone else. Not Beau's son. Not a man who would eventually leave Cool Springs. And her.

"I'm not going to hurt you," he said as if reading her mind. As if he realized the pain she'd experienced losing her mother, her father and a lover who had abandoned her. Her heart was guarded. She'd built up an impenetrable wall of defense against further hurt and pain.

"I can't let you, Brooks."

"I won't. I promise," he said, his gaze dipping to her mouth. She parted her lips and he took her then, in a kiss that was simple and brief and sweet. Moments ticked by as she stared at him, sad regret pulling at her heart. And their fate was sealed. They had come to terms with their attraction and would put a halt to anything leading them astray.

It was quiet in the shed, and cool and dark. Ruby trembled, and that brought her out of her haze. "We should get these boxes into the house. We've got a full day of decorating ahead. Have you seen the tree yet?"

"No, not yet. We should get to it, then."

Brooks got right on it, pulling down two big boxes and loading up his arms while she grabbed one, too. "You know, I haven't decorated for Christmas since I was a kid," he said as they made their way toward the house. "My mom would get this small three-foot tree and put it up on Grandma Gerty's round coffee table. That made it look just as big and tall as the ones we'd see around town. Then Graham and I would put the ornaments on the taller branches, and my little brother, Carson, would decorate the bottom half."

"Did you use tinsel?" she asked, her mood lighter now as she pictured Brooks as a boy.

"My mom always made a popcorn garland. And my grandmother would give us candy canes to stick on the tree."

"My dad and I always used silver tinsel," Ruby said. "It wasn't Christmas until we had the tree covered in it."

"Sounds nice," Brooks said. "I'm sorry Beau isn't going to be decorating with us today. Seems silly now that I'm a grown man, doesn't it?"

"Not at all. You missed out on a lot with Beau. But you know what? I bet before we finish the tree, Beau will come down."

As they entered the massive living room, Brooks took one look at the tree and the ladder beside it and halted his steps, inclining his head. "Wow. Now, that's a tree. Must be a fifteen-footer."

"At least. Every year Beau has the biggest and best Douglas fir delivered to the house. Tanya loved filling up the entire corner of the room with the tree."

They set their boxes down. Brooks scanned the room again and sighed. "It's weird, you know. Having a family here I didn't know about. I'm not complaining. I had a good life. My mother made sure of it. But to think while I was decorating our Christmas tree at home, my father and his family were setting their own Christmas traditions."

"Just think, Brooks. Now you'll have both—a Chicago and a Cool Springs Christmas."

He chuckled. "You're right, Ruby. I guess that's not half-bad."

"No, it's not. Now, here," she said, digging into a box and coming up with a string of large, colorful lights. "Before we can hang any ornaments, we need to make this tree shine. Start at the top and work your way down, Mr. Six-Foot-Two. You've got a lot of catching up to do."

Hours later, Brooks put his arm around Ruby's shoulders as they stepped back from the tree to admire their handiwork. The tree was stunning, the lights in holiday hues casting a soft glimmer over the large formal living room. "It's beautiful," Ruby said quietly.

"It is. We went through six boxes on the tree alone."

"It looks almost perfect," Ruby said, noticing a flaw.

"Almost?"

"Yeah, I see a spot we missed."

"Where?"

She pointed to a bare space toward the top of the tree that had been neglected. "Right there. I'll get it," she said, breaking away from Brooks to grab a beautiful horse ornament, a palomino with a golden mane. "We'll just get this guy up on that branch."

She hugged the side rails of the ladder and began

climbing. Making it to the highest rung, she thought was safe and reached out to a branch just as the ladder wobbled beneath her. "Oh!"

"I've got you," Brooks said, steadying the ladder first and then fitting her butt cheeks into his hands from his stance on the floor.

"Brooks." She swatted at his hands. "Stop that."

"What?" He put innocence in his voice. "I'm only keeping you from falling."

"Shh," she said, her entire body reacting to the grip he had on her. They'd worked together all day long in close quarters, and it was hard enough to keep from touching him, from brushing her body against his, from breathing in his intoxicating scent while trying to focus on the task. "Lupe might hear you. Or Beau might come down."

"Lupe went shopping for groceries, remember? And I heard Beau snoring just a second ago. Doesn't seem like he's going to come down anytime soon."

"Smart aleck. You're got it all figured out, don't you?"

"Hell, I wish I did, Ruby."

She ignored the earnest regret she heard in his voice. "I'm coming down. That means you can take your hands off my ass now."

He grinned and then released her. "I'll be right here, waiting."

"Why does that worry me?" she said as she lowered herself slowly down.

He stood at the base of the ladder, and when she turned around, he was there, crowding her with his body, his scent, his blue beautiful eyes. "I think I have a shelf life around you, Ruby," he said in explanation. "A few hours without touching you is all I can manage."

The compliment seared through her system and warmed all the cold spots. "I know what you mean," she said softly. She felt the same way, and it was useless to deny the attraction.

He gave her a bone-melting smile. "Now, that's honest."

"I'm always honest. Or at least, I try to be."

He held her trapped against the ladder, his arms roped around the sides, blocking her in. When he lowered his head, her eyes closed naturally, and she welcomed his kiss.

"Mmm," she hummed against lips that fit perfectly with hers. Lips that gave so much and demanded even more. The connection she had with Brooks was sharp and swift and powerful. They were like twin magnets that clicked together the minute they got close.

He took her head in his hands and dipped her back, deepening the kiss, probing her with his tongue. He swept inside so quickly she gasped, the pleasure startling her and making her pulse race out of control.

He whispered, "Come to my cabin tonight, Ruby."

"I, uh…" A dozen reasons she shouldn't swarmed into her mind. The same reasons she'd tried to heed before, the same reasons that had kept her up nights.

He kissed her again, meshing their bodies hip to hip, groin to groin. There was no mistaking his erection and the blatant desire pulsing between them. She had to come to terms with wanting Brooks. Not for the future, not because of the past, but for now. In the present. Could she live with that?

"Yes," she said, agreeing to another night with him. "I'll come to you," she promised. And once she said it, her shoulders relaxed and her entire body gave way to relief. She'd put up a good fight, but it was time to realize she couldn't fight what was happening between them. She could only go along for the ride and see where it would take her.

"Ruby, you sure you don't want to watch the end of the game with me and Brooks?" Beau asked from his seat at the head of the dinner table. "We can catch the last half. Looks like the Texans might make the playoffs if they win tonight."

His boys had invited them all to catch the game at the C'mon Inn as they usually did once a week, drinking beer and talking smack, but mother hen that she was, Ruby delicately squashed that idea. Beau needed his rest and some alone time with Brooks, since he'd missed out on being with him today.

"No thanks, Beau. I'll just help Lupe straighten up in the kitchen and then head home. You boys enjoy the game. And remember, don't stay up too late. You may be feeling better, but you still need to turn in early."

"Yes, ma'am, I promise," Beau said, giving her a wink.

He seemed much better than he had this morning. He'd coughed only once during dinner, and his voice had lost that nasal tone. She congratulated herself on getting him to rest today. It had done him a world of good.

"Thanks again to both of you for fixing up the house. Looks real pretty."

"You're welcome." Brooks looked as innocent as a schoolboy as he nodded at his father, but his innocence ended there. He'd been eyeballing Ruby all during dinner, making it hard for her to swallow her food. She was eager to be with him again, to have him nestle her close and make her body come apart.

"It was a lot of fun, Dad. Ruby taught me the finer points of decorating a tree."

Ruby wanted to roll her eyes. Everything Brooks said lately seemed to have a double meaning. Or was she just imagining it?

"She's had enough experience," Beau went on. "She took over from Tanya, you know. And I know my wife would approve of the way you both made the house look so festive. The party's on Saturday night, and son, I can't wait to introduce you to my friends."

"I'll look forward to that."

Beau smiled and then was hit by a sudden fit of coughing. Concerned, Ruby put a hand on his shoulder until he simmered down. "S-sorry," he said.

"Don't apologize, Dad. Maybe I should go so you can turn in early."

"Nah, don't go yet. It's just a tickle. I'm fine."

Beau seemed to recover quickly. He didn't want to miss out on watching football with his son. It was sweet of him, and Brooks seemed to understand.

"All right, then," Brooks said.

"I'm making you a cup of tea, Beau," Ruby said. "No arguments. Go have a seat in the great room and finish the game. I'll bring it in to you. Brooks, would you like some tea?"

"I'll just get myself another beer, if you don't mind. I'll meet you in the other room, Dad."

"Okay, sure," Beau said, heading out.

Brooks cocked his mouth in a smile and followed behind Ruby. When she was almost through the kitchen doorway, his hand snaked out and tugged on her forearm. He spun her around to face him squarely. "What?" she asked, her brows gathering.

"Look up."

She didn't have to. The scent of fresh mistletoe filled her nostrils from above, and before she could comment, Brooks was swooping down, giving her a kiss. It was short-lived, but filled with passion—a kiss that had staying power. "Shelf life," he whispered, searching her face with sea-blue eyes.

"You set me up." He'd put up mistletoe in half a dozen rooms in the house.

"Guilty as charged."

She shoved at his chest, but he didn't budge. "Go," she pleaded. "Watch football with your father." Lupe was clearing the dinner dishes from the dining room table and would be back in the kitchen any second.

"Bossy. I love that about you," he whispered over her lips.

Her skin heated at his seductive words. She pointed toward the great room. "Go. Pleeeze."

He saluted her. "Yes, ma'am. See you soon." Then he turned and walked away.

If he wanted to give her a preview of what was in store for her later that evening, he'd succeeded. The kiss had staying power; it had her nerves jumping and her body primed for his touch.

After delivering a steaming mug of chamomile tea to Beau, she bundled up in a warm wool jacket and exited the house. She was halfway home when her phone rang out—Carrie Underwood again, keying her ex-boyfriend's car.

The screen displayed the caller. "Trace," Ruby muttered.

She couldn't talk to him tonight. She let the call go to voice mail.

But curiosity had her putting the phone to her ear to listen to his message. "Hey, baby. It's Trace. I'm missing you like crazy. I'm coming home tomorrow. I need to see you, babe. We need to talk."

He sounded serious. Trace wanted to talk to her? The entire time they'd dated, he'd put her off about matters of the heart. He'd always said he would rather show her how he felt than ramble off meaningless words. And she'd bought that, hook, line and sinker. For a time, his actions had spoken louder than words. He'd been an attentive boyfriend, showing up with thoughtful gifts, taking her to country music concerts, letting her drive his most prized possession, his fully restored 1964 Ford truck. For a while Ruby had felt like the queen of the world. And she'd fallen hard for him, thinking him the perfect man for her—a man born and raised in Texas, a man who understood her love of horses, a man of the earth.

Together they could enjoy life here in Cool Springs.

But then something had happened. It had started out gradually. Trace had become restless. His attention had drifted. He seemed unsatisfied, as if he needed and wanted more out of life. He was systematically yet subtly pushing her away, and it had taken his being gone for months on the rodeo circuit without calling her for her to realize she'd been dumped. She'd spent many nights crying over him. Wondering what had gone wrong. She'd been in love with him. She'd banked her future on him, and she'd been sucker-punched in the gut when she realized they were truly over.

She'd asked herself if he'd been tired of *her,* or if it was his life that needed a big change. She didn't know, but what she did know was that he didn't want her anymore. Maybe he'd never really loved her. She'd wasted a great deal of time on a man who, in the end, didn't want a future with her.

She wouldn't be that gullible again.

So as she entered her cottage, she showered and changed her clothes and set her mind on keeping her feelings for Brooks neutral. He was a city guy, Beau's long-lost son and a man who'd be leaving town after the holidays. She couldn't give herself fully to Brooks, but she could enjoy spending time with him and look forward to the pleasures they could give each other. Once again she asked herself if her attraction to Brooks was real or simply a way to redeem her blistered and battered soul.

Brooks made her feel feminine and special and beautiful.

That was enough for now.

Shortly after, Ruby parked her car so it was completely hidden from sight behind a feed shed and walked up to Brooks's cabin. She knocked briskly. Her heart was pounding, her mind made up. When Brooks opened the door, she studied the handsome face, the beautiful blue eyes gazing back at her. "My shelf life for you has just expired."

Brooks's eyes flickered, and a growl emanated from his throat.

He took her hand and tugged her inside.

Then slammed the door shut behind them.

Brooks seemed to know. He really seemed to know she didn't need mindless words as he peeled her dress down her arms and over her hips until she was clad only in a pink bra and panties. His groan of approval gave way to him ripping at the buttons of his shirt and yanking it off. Then he lifted her silently, his strong arms under her legs and his mouth covering hers as he moved down the hall. He didn't let up on her lips until they reached the bedroom. His room was bathed in candlelight—a nice touch—and the soft beams delicately caressed the bedsheets.

Instead of lowering her onto the bed, Brooks guided her down his body until her feet met with cool wood floor planks. He reached around and unhooked her bra, then slipped his fingers under the straps, pulling them away and freeing her breasts. He gazed at them for several heartbeats before he hooked her panties with a finger and slid them all the way down her legs. With the slightest move of her feet, she stepped out of them.

It amazed her how much she trusted him. How she allowed him to bear witness to her naked body without worry or shyness. Maybe it was the glow of admiration in his eyes, the way they seemed to touch and warm her at the same time. Her nipples tightened under his scrutiny, and he noticed. "You're cold."

She shook her head no.

She wasn't cold. She was turned on. Ready for whatever Brooks wanted to do.

He walked around her and pressed his body to hers. The length of his manhood rubbed against her backside, and her eyelids lowered ever so slowly. He reached around and cupped her heavy breasts in his hands much like he had her rear end earlier in the day, and then nibbled lustily on the back of her neck. If he was trying to drive her crazy, he was doing a good job. Her body was throbbing now, hot and eager for more.

He wasn't through tormenting her. Next he used his palms to mold her skin from her shoulders down along the very edge of her breasts. He smoothed his hands to the hollow curves of her waist and lower still until his fingertips touched the apex of her thighs, teasing and tempting, bringing her immense pleasure. Instincts had her spreading her legs, welcoming the onslaught, and her breathing escalated. She couldn't think of anything but what he was doing to her. What she wanted him to do to her.

He rubbed against her as he brought her closer still, pressed so tight there was no doubt about his own thick arousal. And then his hand moved to her core, making her gasp and silently plead for more. His fingertips worked the folds of her skin and drew her out with tender but targeted strokes that jolted her body. "Easy now," Brooks whispered as he wrapped his free arm around her waist to steady her while he continued his torment. She was so ready, so primed that it took only a few more infinitely refined strokes to send her sailing over the edge.

She rocked back and shuddered long and hard, the spasms ridiculously powerful. When they were over, Brooks braced her in his arms, bestowing kisses on her shoulders, her back, and then spun her around and looked deep into her eyes.

Ruby was in too much awe to say a word.

Brooks wasn't much in the mood for talking, either. He whipped off his belt and then removed the rest of his clothes. Her eyes dipped to his beautifully ripped and aroused body, and she fell to her knees before him and gave him the same pleasure he'd given her. He groaned from deep in his chest with utter approval, and it wasn't long before he was reaching for her, lifting her up.

"I need to be inside you," he rasped.

"Lie down, Galahad."

And once he was in position, taking up the length of the bed and wearing protection, she threw her leg over his hips and straddled him. "Ah man, Ruby," he said. "You have no idea how you look right now."

"Like I'm about to ride?"

Even through his heated expression, he chuckled. "You comparing me to a horse?"

"Take it as a compliment," she said as she pressed herself down onto him. A low, guttural sigh emerged from his throat as her body took all of him inside. Then she began a slow, steady climb. Brooks's hands were on her hips, holding on or guiding her—she couldn't tell—and then the pace changed, surging and building to a crescendo that had her crying out.

Brooks, too, was there, grunting and sighing in a mix of pain and pleasure.

The climax hit them hard together, and their cries echoed from the cabin walls.

Ruby fell atop him and he gathered her in, holding her tight, cradling her in his arms.

She was spent, her limbs like jelly.

It was a good thing she had Brooks on the brain tonight.

Tomorrow she would have to deal with Trace.

Seven

Ruby stood at the gates of the Cool Springs Christmas Carnival on the outskirts of town. She used to barrel race at these fairgrounds as a young girl. Ruby smiled at the memories. Oh, how she'd always loved it when the carnival came to town. With her father looking on, she'd put her horse through the paces, leaning and reining and guiding those sharp turns, feeling at one with the animal. She'd brought home a few trophies in her day, but once her papa had passed on, Ruby turned to something she loved even more: training horses. It was his legacy that she now carried on at Look Away.

Strings of twinkling lights crisscrossed the carnival grounds. There were giant holly wreaths as well as red-and-green banners announcing the holiday. The chatter of fun-seeking crowds, children's laughter and shouts from hawkers selling cotton candy and funnel cakes brought it all home. Ruby smiled.

It was here that Trace Evans first kissed her, back behind the shack that now sold hot chocolate and coffee. Her heart warmed despite the brisk December night as she stood there taking it all in.

And then she saw him.

Trace.

Approaching from inside the gates, his smile was as broad and sure as she remembered. His polished snakeskin boots leaving dust behind, the six-foot-tall hunk of man worked his way through the crowd as if all the others surrounding him didn't exist, his deep, dark eyes set only on her.

Just like it used to be.

All the worries she'd been plagued with in coming here vanished the instant she laid eyes on him. Seeing Trace, tall in his Stetson, broad in a black-and-white snap-down plaid shirt and giving her a megawatt smile, flooded her senses, and a shiver of warmth ran down her body. Crap. She was here only to put him off. To tell him they were officially over, so that they could both move on with their lives.

She needed to do this face-to-face.

But his *face* was filled with genuine joy. "Ruby," he said, his voice husky and laced with that down-home drawl. "It's good to see you."

She stood there immobilized as he paid for her ticket

and tugged her through the gate. She realized he held her hand, and when she tried to pull away, he drew her up close, bent his head and gave her a quick kiss. "Sorry," he said, dipping his head in that charming way he had. "I've been dreamin' about doing that ever since you agreed to meet me here. Gawd, you look good, Ruby. I've missed you, honey."

"Trace." She put force in her words, ignoring the crazy, mixed-up stirrings in her heart. "I'm here only to—"

"I know, I know. You're not happy with me right now. I get that. How about we enjoy the evening a little before we get all serious? Look over there. Funnel cakes. I'm dying for one. I bet you are, too."

"I, uh…"

"Don't you remember how much we used to crave those things? With all the fixin's, too. Strawberries and whipped cream, the more powdered sugar the better. You game? Come on," he said, taking her hand again. "I'm about to die of starvation."

She rolled her eyes, but a big smile emerged regardless of the company she was in. She was craving a funnel cake, too. They were available only once a year, at this carnival. This was her chance to indulge in a gooey, deep-fried concoction with all the heart-stopping extras. "Okay, sounds good."

"*Delicious* is a better word, sweetheart."

She wasn't his sweetheart and she was ready to tell him, but a few young women and two school-age boys butted into the line, asking Trace for his autograph. He seemed genuinely delighted, giving them each individual attention as he took their names and signed their tickets, flyers, whatever paper article they could produce. Trace had made a name for himself in the field of bull riding. As far as rodeo champions went, he was equivalent to a soap opera star rather than an Academy Award winner, but to the folks around these parts, he was a local hero. Trace ate up all the attention.

"Sorry about that, Ruby," he said, guiding her toward a two-seater café table.

"Do you get that a lot?" she asked, curious now.

"Some," he said, trying for humble, though his grin gave him away. "More and more."

Then his grin faded as his gaze roamed her face, and he sighed from deep in his chest. "I'm sure glad to see you. I've been lonely for you, honey."

"Last I checked, you broke up with me, Trace."

"I never did. Not officially. I, uh, like I told you on the phone, I had to focus on my career, and that meant blocking out everything else."

"That's not exactly comforting, Trace."

She'd felt fully and totally dumped, and there was no way he could salvage what happened between them by using phony excuses.

"Only because being with you was so damn distracting. When we were together, you were all I could ever think about."

He was talking like a man still in love, and if Ruby

was that same gullible girl he'd left behind, she might have swallowed that line again. "When you care for someone, you call. You want to know how they're doing. You—"

"I made mistakes. I'm not denying it." He played with his fork but didn't dig into the funnel cake he craved. "But I'm home now, for good."

"What does that mean, for good?"

"It means I'm gonna stay on in Cool Springs."

"You quit the rodeo?"

He smiled sadly. "I think it quit me, Rube. I'm not cut out for the life. I'm never gonna make it big. Not like I wanted. I gave eight years of my life to the rodeo."

"But you love bull riding." He'd been nineteen when he won his first local rodeo, and the entire town had gotten behind him. Some small businesses in the area sponsored him so he could pursue his dream. It seemed strange to her that he would give it up now. Yes, it was a young man's sport, but he still had years left in him.

"I did. I loved it, but it didn't love me back, Ruby. I gave it my all, and I hope I didn't lose you as a result of my pursuit. I just never got where I wanted to go, and I'm done with all of it. So I'll be home now, just like we'd planned. If I'm lucky enough to win you back, I'm staying put right here."

For her equilibrium's sake, she had to ignore the winning-you-back part. This was all too much to take in. She straightened in her seat to keep from showing her total surprise. "So, what will you do?"

He shrugged. "Dad's getting on in years. He wants me to take over the ranch full-time."

It didn't sound like Trace. He'd always had big plans, and none of them included becoming a local rancher. He was Texan through and through, but Ruby had begun to believe his true heart was elsewhere.

"I saw you on television the other night. *Homestead Hills*?"

"Oh, that. Yeah, I did that on a whim. Met some casting guy at the rodeo who said I'd be perfect in the role. I gave it a try, is all."

"A try?" From what she'd heard, people busted their butts and did all sorts of crazy things to win a role in a hit TV series.

"Nothing much came of it," he said dismissively.

"You haven't touched your funnel cake," she said, finally raising her fork and digging in. The airy pastry, all sugared up, got her taste buds going. When she finally swallowed, a burst of deliciousness slid down her throat. "Mmm, it's good. I shouldn't, but I think I'm going to eat every last bite."

Trace smiled, his gaze focused on her mouth for several beats, and suddenly her insides quaked and her belly quivered. Those familiar yearnings returned. She couldn't believe that one year ago, they'd been doing this very thing: eating funnel cakes and talking about their future.

"Soon as I start," he said, lifting his fork and gazing into her eyes, "this here dessert is gonna be history."

True to his word, Trace demolished his funnel cake.

Ruby wound up leaving half of hers behind. Her stomach was tied in knots once everything Trace had said to her finally sank in. She'd been raised to forgive with an open heart. But would she be a fool to do so?

As they rode the Ferris wheel, circling to the highest point, sitting hip to hip, their legs brushing, they took in the nighttime view of all of Cool Springs, the moon and stars appearing close enough to touch. Trace took her hand, entwining their fingers, and gave her a slight squeeze. In that moment, she saw a glimpse of what life with Trace could be like again.

And a few moments later, Trace set his money down at a gaming booth and wasn't satisfied until he hit the bull's-eye target with a dart gun to win her an adorable stuffed reindeer. "Here you go, miss," he said, bowing and presenting her with the toy.

He used to be her hero.

Could he be again?

She was as confused as ever, with the Trace she remembered returning to her and saying all the right things, making her feel like she mattered to him. She was a long way from forgiving him…and then there was Brooks.

A sigh blew from her lips, and Trace turned to her. "What?"

She shook her head. "Nothing. I should go."

"You sure? We haven't gone into Santa's Village yet."

"I'm sure."

Disappointment dimmed the gleam in his eyes. "Okay, I'll walk you to your car."

He took hold of her hand again. She didn't want to make a fuss by pulling free of him, so they walked hand in hand into the parking lot.

Now's your chance. Tell him you're not taking him back. Tell him he hurt you and...

The words didn't come. She couldn't yank them out of her throat. Not when he was being so dang sweet and trying so hard to impress her.

When they reached her car, she hoped to make a quick getaway. Launching into her handbag for her key fob, she moved away from him, breaking their connection. "Good night, Trace. Thanks for the funnel cake," she said, opening the car door.

He glanced at her hand on the door handle and knew enough not to press her tonight. "I'll call you tomorrow."

She should tell him no. There was no point. "Okay."

Before he could say anything more, she slid into the seat and pressed the ignition button.

The car didn't rev right up. In fact, nothing happened. She pressed the button again, giving the engine gas.

Again nothing.

Shoot. Trace walked over. He had a keen sense of cars, and judging by the expression on his face, this couldn't be good. After fiddling with the ignition button, he spent a few minutes under the hood and came up looking bleak. "You want the good news or the bad news?"

"Bad."

"The car's not going anywhere tonight. Not without a tow."

Ruby silently cursed under her breath.

"The good news is, I can give you a lift home."

Parked in front of her cottage now, Ruby slid across the pristine leather seat, angling for the truck's door handle. "Thanks for the ride, Trace." Her head was spinning from spending time with him tonight. It was almost too much to take in. What they had once was pretty darn remarkable. Being with him tonight at the carnival had brought back memories of the good times they'd shared when Trace had loved her.

Before he'd had second thoughts.

Before he'd turned into a jerk.

"Hold up a sec, Ruby." The urgency in his voice stilled her. He climbed out of his truck and spun around the hood to open the door for her. He offered his hand, and she fitted her palm inside his as she stepped out. Now that they were alone under beautiful moonlight, she waited for the butterflies to attack her stomach, but nothing seemed to happen. No flip-flops. No queasy feeling. No little bursts of excitement.

That was a good thing, right?

As soon as her boots landed on Preston soil, she pulled her hand free, grabbing for her purse, ready to end this night. Earlier, rather than have her wait for a tow, Trace had insisted on taking her home. His good buddy Randy over at Cool Springs Auto promised to tow her car to the shop and take a look at it first thing in the morning. Ruby couldn't argue with that logic. She would've had to do the same thing, and Trace had effortlessly taken care of everything for her.

Ruby had always thought of herself as an independent woman. She could fend for herself, but having Trace take over the reins tonight and deal with her car issues was nice for a change.

"I'll walk you to your door," he said.

She didn't like the prospect of Trace giving her a good-night kiss, one more potent than the one he'd given her at the festival. He'd been her first love, and the splinters of his betrayal were still stabbing her. The pain wasn't as strong as it had once been, but it left behind scars that had yet to heal. She couldn't be a fool twice. "There's no need, Trace." Her door was ten feet away, and having him walk her there implied much more than she was willing to concede right now.

"Okay. But before you go, Ruby, I, uh…"

Brisk night breezes put a chill in her bones as she faced him, her back against the bed of the truck. He stepped closer and removed his hat, hesitating as if searching for the right words. Whatever he had to say had to be important for him to stumble this way. Usually confident, he rubbed at the back of his neck and inhaled from deep in his chest. She'd never seen him quite like this, and she almost wanted to put a hand on his arm to steady him. Almost.

"I wanted to say I'm sorry…deeply sorry for the way I treated you. I should've realized what we had was special, and now that I'm home to stay, I want to make it up to you. I want to start fresh. You and me, we were good together. I want that—"

The sound of footsteps crunching gravel came from the road behind them. She swiveled her head as a figure came out of the shadows and into the ring of moonlight surrounding them.

Trace saw him, too. "Who in hell is that?" he asked none too quietly.

Ruby tried not to react. "Beau's son."

Now that Brooks was upon them, his brows arched as his inquisitive glance went from her to Trace and back again. "Evenin'," he said. He was picking up a Texas drawl, probably from spending time with Beau. She almost chuckled, except seeing her ex-boyfriend meet up with her current lover wasn't a laughing matter.

"Hi, Brooks." There was cheery lightness in her voice worthy of a big Hollywood award.

"Ruby."

"Oh, um, Brooks, I'd like you to meet Trace Evans. Trace, this is one of Beau's twin sons, Brooks. He's visiting here from Chicago, getting to know the family."

Trace sized Brooks up as he put out his hand. "Nice meetin' ya."

"Same here," Brooks said without much enthusiasm as the two pumped hands.

"So, you're one of the lost boys Beau's been searching for. I heard about you. Not from Ruby, though. She didn't say a word about you all night, but word spreads quickly when someone new shows up in Cool Springs."

"I met Trace at the Christmas carnival in town," she was quick to explain. "My car broke down and Trace offered me a lift home."

Trace took a place beside Ruby against the truck. "Yeah, just like old times. Ruby and I go back a ways. Don't know if she told you about us, but I'm back in town now." He gave Brooks a smile. Was he warning Brooks off or simply making conversation? Trace had no reason to suspect anything, not that it mattered anyway. He didn't have a claim on her anymore. "So, how are you liking Cool Springs so far?" he asked.

"I'm liking it just fine." Brooks said the words slowly, giving nothing away by his tone. Yet his gaze shifted to her every so often as if puzzling out what was happening. "I'm beginning to feel right at home here at Look Away."

Ruby edged away from Trace. If he put his arm around her to haul her closer, she'd cringe.

"Must be, if you're out taking a walk this time of night in the cool air."

"I'm used to cold weather. Chicago winters can be brutal. Actually, I wasn't out walking for the sake of walking. I came to ask Ruby a favor. Is all," he added.

Ruby kept her lips buttoned. Brooks playing the country bumpkin was enough to make her laugh. But she didn't dare.

"That so?" Trace asked.

"Yeah."

"Ruby and I were in the middle of a conversation," Trace announced, as if that wasn't obvious.

"Was I interrupting?" A choir boy couldn't have appeared more innocent.

"You were, actually," Trace replied, his chest expanding as he stood a bit taller.

This was not going well, and it was clear Brooks wasn't going to back down.

"Don't let me stop you," Trace said, gesturing with a royal sweep of his arm. "Go ahead and ask Ruby your favor."

"Actually Trace, I'm not up for this conversation tonight," Ruby said. "It's been a long day, and I'm tired. Brooks, can your question wait until tomorrow?"

He glanced at Trace, eyeing him for a second before nodding. "Sure thing. It can wait."

"Okay, then. We'll talk tomorrow. And Trace, thanks again for the lift."

"You're welcome. I enjoyed our date, honey."

It wouldn't do any good denying it was date. Trace had it in his head it was.

Both men stood like statues, refusing to move.

"Well, good night, then." She made her way past Trace and rolled her eyes at Brooks as she brushed by him. His lips twitched in amusement, and for that split second, devilish images of tossing him over her shoulder played out in her head.

She left them both standing there and walked to her door. Curiosity had her turning around briefly to see Trace waiting until Brooks was well on his way before getting into his truck and starting the engine.

Men.

"So what's with your ex showing up?" Brooks wasted no time with pleasantries, yet his tone coming through her cell phone was more curious than accusatory.

"Where are you?" It hadn't been but ten minutes since he'd left her. Cozy in her pajamas and tucked into bed already, she really was unusually tired tonight and…confused. She hadn't expected the man she'd banked all her dreams on once to show up with apologies and promises.

Promises that she'd waited so long to hear.

"I'm at my place. Sitting here wondering what's going on with you. Are you okay?"

"I'm okay. It wasn't really a date, Brooks. Trace wanted to talk to me and apologize, I guess. I agreed to meet him at the Christmas carnival."

"So, are you forgiving him?"

"I don't know what I am at the moment, Brooks."

The line went silent. A moment ticked by, and then a sigh came through. "Is it none of my business?"

Now, that also was unexpected. Brooks had a way

of getting to the heart of the matter. "It may be your business, a little, since we've been seeing each other."

She hadn't had to deal with the reality of their relationship until now. But it was evident Brooks had made her no promises and he was bound to leave for Chicago after the holidays, while Trace was offering her something that she'd always wanted. "I want to continue seeing you, Ruby."

"I, uh, I just don't know, Brooks." Could she be blunt and tell him she couldn't afford to get her heart broken again if she gave in to her feelings for him and he left town? Could she tell him that he hadn't offered her the sun, the moon and the stars the way Trace once had? It was silly to think Brooks would. They'd known each other only a couple of weeks. Though things had been humming along very smoothly until Trace showed up. "I can't be pressured right now."

"I don't want to pressure you, Ruby. But this guy's hurt you once, and I wouldn't want to see that happen again. I care about you."

"I care about you, too, Brooks. But we both know..." She hesitated, biting her lip, searching for a way to put it that wouldn't seem callous or crude. The truth was, they were hot for each other. They'd had a chance meeting in a bar—the cliché hook-up—and it would've ended there if Brooks hadn't turned out to be a Preston. Now they couldn't seem to keep their hands off each other.

"What do we know?" he asked.

"We've been thrown together under strange circumstances, wouldn't you say?"

"I suppose. When I first met you, I never once thought you'd be a part of the Preston family. Shoot, it blew my mind when you walked into the barn that day. But I'm not sorry you did. Are you?"

The truth was, no. She wasn't sorry she'd met Brooks. She liked him, and maybe her feelings went much deeper than that, but she wouldn't face them. She couldn't. It wasn't just because he was Beau's son. Or because of all of the secrecy and guilt involved in seeing Brooks. No, she couldn't face deeper feelings because her heart wasn't healed enough to let another man inside. So even though she'd slept with Brooks, readily giving him her body, she'd held a small part of herself back. She couldn't give herself wholly to him, and at this point, he hadn't asked that of her, either. "No, I'm not sorry." Enough said for now on the subject. And because her curiosity was tapped, she asked, "Did you really come by to ask me a favor, or was that a little fib?"

"No fib. Although I'll admit, I wanted to see you tonight." His voice turned husky, and whenever it deepened like that, she melted a little inside.

"Did you want to go out for another ride tomorrow or something?"

"I'd love to. But that's not the favor. The truth is, I've been thinking about my grandfather. I need to make my peace about him, and I've been putting off a visit to his nursing home. I'm not sure I'm ready to go it alone and face him. That man caused my family a lot of grief, and I don't know how I'm going to react. But I need to put it behind me so I can move on."

"Would you like me to go with you, Brooks?"

His relief came in the way of a quick sigh. "Would you?"

"Yes, of course. I'll go with you whenever you want."

"Really? That's great. I'm... I'm thinking I'll arrange an appointment sometime before the holiday party this weekend. I want to—"

"I'll clear my calendar whenever you can arrange it."

"Okay," he said, his voice cracking a little. As if he was barely holding it together, as if this visit to his grandfather had been festering in his mind. "It means a lot." Breath whooshed out of his lungs. "Thank you, Ruby."

"Of course."

Sadness swept through her when she heard the pain in Brooks's voice. It only served to prove how much she cared about him. If she could do anything to bring him some peace and sense of closure, she was right on it. But it was more than that. She wanted to be by Brooks's side, to give him the support and encouragement he might need to make that visit easier for him.

He was her friend, at the very least.

Eight

Brooks stood shoulder to shoulder with Beau on the steps of the ranch house as a black limo pulled up and parked. His father took a deep breath in anticipation of seeing his other son for the first time. "I'm the better-looking twin," Brooks said, smiling.

Beau's chuckle caught in his throat as Graham stepped out of the car. "My God."

"Yeah, I know." It was the typical reaction people had when they met the Newport twins for the first time. One face on two very different men. "Graham cut his hair a bit shorter than usual just so you could tell us apart."

"That's...smart," Beau said with a catch in his throat. Then he took off straight toward the limo, and Brooks followed.

Graham was reaching inside the limo to help his fiancée out of the car. It had been a while since Brooks
had seen Eve Winchester. Because she was Sutton Winchester's daughter, she'd been an immediate adversary,
and he hadn't liked her for a time, but Graham was head
over heels in love with Eve, and Brooks had finally
made his peace with her.

"Welcome, son," Beau said, trying his best to keep
his composure. As Brooks sidled up next to him, he
spotted tears glistening in his father's eyes. "I've waited
a long time to meet you."

"So have I."

The two men embraced, and Brooks gave Eve a smile
and a peck on the cheek.

Graham broke away first from the bear hug, taking
Eve's hand and gently tugging her forward.

"Beau, I'd like you to meet Eve. My fiancée," Graham said.

Beau embraced Eve carefully. Despite the beige
leather jacket and blouse underneath, Eve's baby
bump couldn't be missed on her slender, athletic body.
"Pleased you meet you, Eve. Welcome to my home, and
congratulations on the little one. I couldn't be happier
about all of this. My two sons, a new soon-to-be daughter and a grandbaby on the way."

"We're excited about it, too," Graham said, and there
were smiles all around.

"I'd appreciate it if both of you called me Dad."

Graham shot Brooks a quick glance as if to say, *Fi-*

nally. We have a dad. "I think we'd both like to do that, right Eve?"

Her green eyes glittered. "Yes, of course."

Beau's lips curved up in a wide smile. Then he scratched his head, shifting his gaze from Graham to Brooks. "You two boys are certainly identical. That much can't be denied."

"No, but I've wanted to deny this guy was my brother a time or two," Graham said, eyes twinkling. It was meant as a joke, but there was some truth there, too. They'd had their differences, especially lately. Graham hadn't exactly approved of the tactics Brooks had used to go after Sutton Winchester.

"Is that so?" Beau asked, puzzled.

"But it's all good now, right Graham?" Brooks was quick to point out.

"Right." His brother had the good grace to nod and agree. Brooks didn't want to dredge up the past, not now, when they'd finally found their family. It was all about the future now.

"Graham, I've gotten a chance to get to know Brooks, and he's told me some about the two of you growing up. I can't wait to get to know more about you and get acquainted with Eve. I have to admit…there was a time when I didn't t-think this day…would e-ever come." Beau choked up.

Graham's eyes watered a little, too. "Well, we're here now for a few days and we'll have lots of time to catch up."

"You'll stay for the holiday?"

"Of course."

"I'm happy to have you here for as long as you want. Let's get out of the weather. Come on inside. I'll show you to your room."

The chauffeur brought the bags in behind his family as they entered the house, but Brooks held back. There was something missing, or rather, *someone*.

He did a quick scan of the grounds, looking for signs of Ruby. Since their conversation two days ago, he hadn't stopped thinking about her or his reaction to seeing her with Trace Evans. Jealousy had surged as strong as he'd ever felt it, making him stop and assess exactly what was going on between him and Ruby. He'd never met a woman quite like her, and the thought of her going back to her ex put an ache in his gut.

His hands were tied right now. Ruby didn't want anyone to find out about their affair, and he couldn't openly date her. But he wanted to. And that surprised him. He'd never let a woman get close to him. He'd dated, but only halfheartedly and without any notion of commitment. He'd been married to his work and, more recently, too obsessed with finding his true parentage to pursue anyone seriously.

In the back of his mind, he'd always thought that if he met the right woman, all things would fall into place. That had never happened.

With Ruby, it wasn't just about sex. He'd figured that out straightaway. It wasn't even that she was forbidden in every sense of the word. Although that had been dangerously exciting. Everything about her seemed to turn him on. Her independence. Her spunk. The way she never gave in or gave up.

But love and romance had taken a backseat in his life lately, and he couldn't trust what he was feeling. He was out of his element here on Look Away and more vulnerable than he'd ever been before. Yet the more comfortable he was becoming on the ranch, the more he could begin to see himself with Ruby Lopez.

That's why he'd picked up the phone yesterday and placed a call to Roman Slater to find out more about Trace Evans. A secret little investigation from his friend, a top-notch PI, seemed in order. Brooks had a feeling Trace wasn't what he seemed. Beau didn't have a good opinion of the guy, either, and the last thing Brooks wanted was for Ruby to get hurt again.

Then his gaze hit upon the beautiful raven-haired Latina approaching the barn some distance away, and just seeing her again sent his pulse racing. Dressed in a black quilted vest, skin-tight jeans and tall riding boots, she was a vision in her work clothes. He couldn't believe how badly he wanted to be there when she met his brother. He wanted to be the one to introduce them.

"Ruby," he called out as he began to take long strides in her direction.

She'd finally spotted him and stopped in her tracks, staring at him from just outside the barn.

"Ruby," he said again, more softly this time, as he finally came face-to-face with her.

"Hi, Brooks." Her almond-shaped eyes widened in a curious stare, waiting for him to speak.

"Hi." He smiled like an idiot. He couldn't even pretend to be cool around her anymore. "Good seeing you."

She nodded but said nothing more. Yet the question in her eyes gave him pause.

"Are you working this afternoon?" he asked.

"Yeah, I was planning on taking Spirit out. Why?"

"My brother's here with his fiancée. They just arrived. I wanted to introduce you."

"Right now?"

He shrugged. He felt like an ass. And Ruby was trying not to look at him as if he'd lost his mind. Beau had invited everyone for dinner tonight to meet Eve and Graham, and as far as Brooks knew, all of the half brothers and Ruby were coming. "Well, yeah. I want you to meet Graham and Eve right now."

Ruby's brows drew together. "It's important to you?"

"It'll take only a minute or two, and yeah, it's important to me." Ruby was becoming *important* to him, more and more. It had taken seeing her with her ex to make him realize it. He was having some heavy-duty trepidation about his relationship with her and where it was going. Or not going. He'd grown up in a small family, without a father figure to look up to and sharing this part of himself with her meant a great deal to him.

Ruby eyed him for a short while, making up her mind, and then nodded. "I can do that."

"Okay, great." He wanted to wrap her up in his arms and kiss her senseless right there on the spot. He wanted to tell her she was more than a fling to him, more than a secret affair. She was beginning to fill up the voids inside him that he hadn't even known were there. But now was not the time to tell her.

"I'll just go to my place and change."

"Change? Good God, Ruby." He took in that shining sheet of black hair, those incredible cocoa eyes, the way her clothes hugged her body. "You don't need to change a thing. You're perfect just the way you are." He put out his hand. "Come with me?"

She flushed pink at his compliment. "Galahad. You do have a way about you."

And when Ruby put her hand in his, a sense of peace settled over him.

The introductions had gone well yesterday and Brooks was glad of it. Who knew Eve and Ruby would hit it off so well? The pretty green-eyed president of Elite Industries, soon to be his new sister-in-law, and Ruby, horse trainer extraordinaire, had talked fashion, country rock music, Cool Springs versus Chicago, and football, of all things. And because Graham and his fiancée were anxious to see some local Texas color, he and Ruby had brought them to the C'mon Inn for drinks tonight.

Now, as the Newport brothers nursed their whiskeys at the very place Brooks first set eyes on Ruby, the girls chatted and filled the corner booth with bright laughter. Both women were beyond pretty. Both were strong-willed and determined and accomplished.

Sitting beside his fiancée, Graham reached for Eve's hand, claiming the woman as his, while Brooks looked on, wishing he could do the same with Ruby. His brother kept his eyes on Ruby and him, and that twin thing happened. Graham had figured out something was up. Brooks would be hearing about it later. Graham wasn't one to keep his thoughts to himself.

The conversation turned to the feud between the Winchesters and the Newports, and Eve was trying to put things as delicately as she could. "So, you see, Brooks had this vendetta against my father and dug up some dirt—that proved not to be true, by the way—and went to the media to reveal the whole sordid scandal."

Ruby's gaze fell solidly on him. "That doesn't sound like Brooks."

"How well do you know my brother?" Graham was teasing, but the comment fell flat.

"I thought I knew him well enough," she answered.

"It's a long story and the bottom line is, we've resolved those differences," Brooks said in his own defense. "Haven't we, Eve?"

The uncertain look in Ruby's eyes was knifing through his gut. What she thought of him mattered, and he didn't want to lose his Galahad status with her. At the time, he'd had good reason to go after Winchester, but that was over and done with, and he'd made his peace with his brother's fiancée.

Eve was cordial enough to agree. "Yes. Thanks to Graham. He took back all the allegations and, well, stole my heart in the process. But I will confess that Brooks thought he was justified in going after my father. For a time, it was thought that my dad, Sutton, could've fathered the twins, since he and their mother had been in love. And Brooks thought Sutton was hiding something."

"As it turned out, Sutton is our younger brother's father," Graham said. "But our mom hid that pregnancy from Sutton and moved on with her life. He only recently found out Carson was his son."

Brooks sipped whiskey. The entire mess that was his life these past few years was coming to light. He wasn't ashamed of his actions—he'd thought he had good reason—but if he had to do it over again, he might've done some things differently.

His obsession with Sutton Winchester was coming to a close. The man was dying, and there'd been enough grief and heartache already over the mistakes and actions of the many people involved. It wasn't just Sutton. Brooks's mother wasn't entirely faultless. Nor was his Grandma Gerty. There was enough blame to go around.

"Well," Graham said. "It all turned out okay since I now have Eve and a baby on the way. So something wonderful came of all of it."

Brooks raised his glass. "I'll drink to that."

Graham brought his tumbler up, and the women raised their iced tea glasses.

"To family," Brooks said, staring into Ruby's eyes.

"To family," they all parroted, and then clinked glasses and sipped their drinks.

"Ruby, would you like something stronger?" Brooks asked.

"No thanks. I think I'll lay off tonight. I ate too much of Lupe's tamale pie at dinner."

"Gosh, me, too. It was delicious," Graham said, patting his stomach. "I hear you're a pretty good pool player, Ruby."

"She's a hustler," Brooks said, grinning.

"Is that right? Eve's pretty good, too."

The women exchanged glances.

"Want to?" Ruby asked.

"Sounds like fun," Eve replied.

"This I gotta see." Graham rose from his seat to let Eve scoot out.

Brooks did the same, and Ruby's exotic flowery scent wafted to his nose as she brushed by him. His lust had to give way to decorum. He and Ruby were in a standoff right now, and he doubted she'd be inviting him into her bed anytime soon.

The women headed to the pool table at the back of the room, secured pool sticks and cued up as Brooks and his brother leaned against the far wall. "Go easy on her, Ruby," Brooks called. "She's a guest in Cool Springs."

"Go easy, nothing," Eve countered, the fierceness in her eyes indicating she was ready for battle. "Don't hold back, Ruby. I can handle it."

Graham chuckled and said quietly, "She can. She's pretty amazing."

"It's good to see you happy, bro."

"Yeah, I am. I managed not to blow it with Eve. Thank God for that. And meeting Beau was pretty great, too. I wasn't sure about any of this, coming here to Texas and being brought into a whole new family. But Beau's made it real easy. He's a good man, and there was no awkwardness between us."

"Because I paved the way," Brooks said, giving his brother grief. "As usual."

"Smart-ass. So what's with you and Ruby? And don't tell me nothing's going on. I can practically see the steam rising between the two of you from across the booth. Have you fallen for her?"

Brooks drew oxygen into his lungs and kept his voice low. The women were preoccupied; Eve was about to make the first shot. "I'm in the process, I think." What the hell kind of answer was that? He was in the process of falling for her? While trying to keep things light with Ruby, it had gotten hot and heavy real fast. "It's complicated."

"I hear you. Couldn't be more complicated than me falling for Winchester's daughter, now, could it?"

"I don't know about that. Ruby's like a daughter to

Beau, and if I hurt her, there'll be hell to pay. Not exactly the impression I want to make on our father."

"Hell, man. Make it a priority not to hurt her, then."

Brooks stared at his brother, letting his words sink in. Was it that easy? Did he want Ruby? He darted a glance at her. She was taking aim, her hot body stretched across the pool table, her eyes laser-focused, her kissable mouth pursed tight as she drew back the stick and *clack*, the cue ball sailed across the table and hit its mark. The striped ball dropped into the side pocket.

Hell yeah, he wanted Ruby. From the moment he'd first laid eyes on her right here at the C'mon Inn, he'd been drawn to her. She had substance and class and a sassy mouth that made him smile, even when that sass was aimed at him. He admired her passion and knowledge of horses and her open method of teaching that came straight from the heart. He couldn't imagine not seeing her day in and day out. Not speaking to her and not laughing with her. Up until this moment, he hadn't thought about the time when he'd have to go back to Chicago for good.

He'd never been really serious about a woman before. For one, he'd been preoccupied with work, striving for and finally attaining the financial independence he'd craved ever since the more humble days of his youth. He'd worked hard building the Newport Corporation and didn't have time to play much. As a result, women had come and gone in his life. Rightfully so. He hadn't been ready for a strong commitment. He had only so much to give, and getting serious with the opposite sex had taken a backseat to all else. More recently, he'd been too caught up in meeting his father after years of searching to let his mind go anywhere else. But now that he was faced with the possibility of losing Ruby to her ex-boyfriend, he had to make a stand.

Sooner rather than later.

But first, there was something he had to do.

And he wanted Ruby by his side.

Hutchinson's Nursing Home, twenty miles outside Cool Springs, sat nestled inside brick walls and a set of wrought iron gates. The grounds were groomed carefully. Right now, the cold Texas weather prevented any flowers from blooming in the beds next to the long, sweeping veranda, but Ruby could picture them thriving there in the spring, their color cheering up the dementia patients who would sit in patio chairs outside to get a little air.

Brooks rested his arms on the steering wheel, staring at the large mansion-like brick home with its pretty white shutters. He sighed. "This is it."

It wasn't going to be a loving homecoming, this much Ruby knew. But she understood his need to come here for closure, while his brother Graham had no desire to meet his grandfather. The twins may have looked exactly alike, but they were two very different men in the way they dealt with life.

Ruby reached for Brooks's hand and squeezed. "We

can make this quick," she said. "And I'll be with you every step of the way."

"Thanks." Brooks rubbed the back of his neck and gave her a solemn look. "I don't think I could do this without you." His blue eyes melted her heart. She felt honored and a little awed that Brooks had counted on her so much. That he needed her.

It was one thing to be wanted.

But to be needed by such a strong man was something else entirely.

"I'm here, Brooks. Let's go meet your grandfather."

Once they were inside a few minutes later, a nurse escorted them to the visitors' room, where they were told to stand just inside the doorway. The woman walked over to a man with a shock of pearl-gray hair seated by a window and spoke a few words to him. He barely acknowledged her, but he turned his head slightly to the door, his expression blank but for a sliver of light entering his eyes.

Ruby felt Brooks freeze up, his body stiffening. He closed his eyes, and she tightened her hold on his hand. "It's going to be okay," she whispered.

"Yeah," he said quietly, but he hesitated.

The nurse waved them over and placed two chairs by the window to face the old man, who was slumped over in his seat.

"Ready?" Ruby asked.

Brooks nodded. She was by his side as they walked over and sat down.

"Hello," Ruby said first. "I'm Ruby."

"You're a pretty thing," the old man said in a child-like voice. "I don't know you, do I?"

Ruby shook her head. "No."

He blinked and seemed to stare straight through her.

The nurse put her hand on Bill Turner's shoulder. "Mr. Turner, this is your grandson, Brooks."

"My grandson?" Bill stared blankly at Brooks. "I don't have a grandson."

"You have two grandsons," Brooks said. "Twins. I have a brother named Graham."

As the nurse walked off, the man began shaking his head.

"They are your daughter Mary Jo's children," Ruby offered.

At the mention of Mary Jo, Bill Turner's eyes switched on. "My daughter? She sits by the fireplace and reads. She likes to read. Quiet little girl. Where is Mary Jo? Is she coming?"

"No, she's not coming today," Brooks said, moisture pooling in his eyes.

Ruby ached inside as she watched Brooks swipe at his tears.

"Maybe she'll come another day," the old man said. "I would like to see her."

"Maybe she will," Ruby said. "How do you like it here, Mr. Turner?"

He shrugged. "I guess I like it fine."

"The people seem nice."

"Where's Mary Jo?" He looked toward the doorway. "She likes to read. Her nose is always in a book. She's a smart girl."

"She is a smart girl," Brooks managed to answer. "And s-she loves to read."

"Do I know you?" Bill Turner's brows gathered. The wrinkles and blankness on his face hid the handsome man he'd once been. "I don't think I know you."

"No," Brooks said, his gaze turning Ruby's way, hopelessness in his expression. He tried again. "You don't know me. But I'm your grandson. Mary Jo was my mother. You are my grandfather."

He shot Brooks another blank stare. "I'm your grandfather?"

Brooks nodded. "Yes."

Bill Turner looked out the window, focusing on a bird hopping on the ground beside a mesquite tree just a few yards away.

"Mr. Turner?" Ruby put her hand on his arm.

He swiveled his head slowly back to them. "I used to build things, you know. I built my own house. This is not my house. I didn't build this."

"No, but it's your home now, Mr. Turner," Ruby said quietly.

"Yes. It's my home now." The light in his eyes dimmed. Then he popped his head up, in search of the nurse. "I think it's time for lunch."

Brooks stared at him for several heartbeats, then sighed and rose from the chair. Ruby witnessed a depth of sadness and pain in his eyes she'd never seen before. "We have to go now, Mr. Turner," he said, taking Ruby's hand again. "Have a good lunch."

They exited without saying another word, and Brooks stopped as they reached his parked car. "It's so damn unfair."

"What?" Her stomach churned. She could guess what Brooks was about to say.

"He's like a child. He doesn't remember his abuse. He doesn't remember hurting his family. He's blacked out the bad times."

"You're angry," Ruby said.

"I'm…yeah, I guess I'm pretty pissed. I wanted to meet the son of a bitch and lay into him about my mother. Someone needed to defend her and look out for her. Someone had to stand up to him. Even though I'm years late, I had it in my head I'd come here and tell the old guy off." He fisted his hands. "But he's in a world of his own. Nothing I'd say to him would sink in."

"Probably not, Brooks. That's the sad thing about dementia. He's trapped in his own head," Ruby said.

Brooks dropped his gaze to the ground, shaking his head.

Ruby stepped closer and stared into his handsome face, which was tightly lined in raw pain. He was fighting to keep the tears away. "It's okay to feel all the things you're feeling. Coming here will give you closure, trust me. It will. When you get back home and think about this, you'll feel better. You'll begin to feel whole again."

Brooks slowly wrapped his arms around her waist and drew her closer. She laid her head on his chest. His heart was beating so fast she placed her hand there to calm him, to give him the balm he needed right now. Nestled in his embrace, she waited for the beats to slow to a normal pace.

"How come you know me so well, Ruby?" He brushed the top of her head with a kiss.

"I just do, I guess."

He tightened his hold, locking her against his body as they swayed ever so slightly together to the music. Electricity sizzled. It always did when they were this close. "You feel so damn good in my arms."

"Humph."

"I didn't mean it that way."

"I know how you meant it, Brooks." He welcomed her comfort. He needed her here, and she wouldn't want it any other way. "I'm just giving you jazz."

"Because that's what you do."

"Yeah, that's what I do."

"Don't ever stop doing that," he whispered into her ear.

Something fierce and protective crackled and snapped inside her. And in that moment, Ruby knew she never wanted to stop giving him *anything*. She'd fallen in love with him. She loved him so much, she wanted to take away his pain, absorb it and tuck it away in some deep, dark place, never to return. She loved Brooks Newport.

But did she still love Trace, too?

Right now, in Brooks's arms, she was giving him all he needed. She wouldn't think about the future and the fact that Brooks would be leaving after the holidays.

He had a home in Chicago.

A thriving business there.

And none of it included her.

The next day, Ruby licked around her cone of dark chocolate fudge ice cream, enjoying every second of her indulgence. Sitting beside her at the Fudge You Ice Cream Factory, Eve was doing the same, digging into her chocolate cone, and Serena, who was happy to join them today, sat across the booth, devouring a dish of French vanilla scoops topped with caramel sauce.

"Yum," Eve said, crunching down on the sugar cone. "I can't remember the last time I had ice cream."

"You don't crave ice cream?" Serena asked. "Isn't that the go-to craving when you're pregnant?"

"That's what I hear. But for me it's more potato chips and dip. Give me salt and I'm happy. But I'd never turn down good ice cream. If I don't watch it, I'll be floating away like a balloon soon."

"Eve, you look fantastic. You don't have to watch anything," Ruby said, hiding the fact that it was her craving for ice cream and not Eve's that had brought them here today.

Eve chuckled. "Thanks for that. The ice cream is amazing. And so is the company." Eve smiled at both of them.

"It's your reward for beating me at pool," Ruby added. "I told you if you won, I'd have something fun in store for you." Fun and indulgent. Ruby needed that, too, now more than ever. Coming here with Eve and Serena was much better than suffering alone at her cottage and digging into a pint or two of decadent ice cream in front of the television set, pining over the state of her love life.

How could one man make her so happy and so sad at the same time?

Brooks had been hurting yesterday and it was only natural for her to comfort him, to allow him time to grieve over his grandfather…because that's exactly what he had done. He'd met Bill Turner for the first time and said farewell to the old man, probably never to see him again, all in one afternoon. The ordeal had shaken Brooks, and seeing him that way had sent her own wobbly emotions out of whack.

"Actually, it's really sweet of you to entertain me today while Graham and Brooks are out riding with Beau," Eve said. "Graham couldn't wait to ride on one of his dad's Thoroughbreds."

Ruby turned her attention back to the girls. "Are you kidding? My stomach is doing somersaults right now. It's been too long since I've had Fudge You ice cream. I'm happy to do it."

"This does beat eating lunch," Serena said. "I'm glad I'm on winter break right now so I could join you."

"Serena is the new principal of Cool Springs High School," Ruby explained to Eve. "The kids love her over there. She's made going to the principal's office a cool thing."

"Oh, really? How so?" Eve asked, her brows lifting as she turned to Serena.

"Well, there are still times it sucks getting summoned to the principal's office," Serena said, "but now, if students do something remarkable like helping a fellow student out of a jam or achieving higher grades than expected because of hard work, I reward them."

"She takes them to lunch," Ruby said, "or lets them skip gym for a week, or gives them a season pass to the football games."

"Among other things," Serena said. "It gives the kids an incentive to do well. They seem to like it."

"They sure do," Ruby said, praising her friend. "And they like Serena a whole helluva lot more than we cared for Mr. Hale, our principal back in the day. That man never cracked a smile."

"I like your creative approach," Eve said. "I can see why the kids adore you."

Ruby gobbled up her cone before the girls were halfway through theirs. She gazed longingly at the mounds of ice cream under the glass case, wishing she could have another cone or maybe a sundae with whipped cream and cherries on top. What was wrong with her?

Even with the Trace-and-Brooks-induced stomachache she'd had lately, her appetite was voracious.

Too soon, all the cones were history, and Serena was rising from her seat. "Sorry to dash out, but I've got an errand list a mile long for this afternoon. It was nice meeting you, Eve. I hope to see you again."

"Same here, Serena," Eve said. "I'm glad you joined us."

"Serena's coming to Look Away for our Christmas party, so you'll see her again," Ruby said.

"That's great," Eve said. "Well then, I'll see you in a few days."

"I'm looking forward to it. Bye girls." Serena exited the shop.

"She's nice," Eve said. "You've been friends a long time?"

"We have. Serena's like a sister to me."

"And Beau's like a father."

"He is. He's a good man. I'm fortunate to have the Prestons. We're pretty tight."

Eve sipped water and smiled. "I can see that. It's really refreshing. My family…well, we've had our differences. But my sisters and I are close. You know, in a sense, you and I will be sisters, too. In-laws, but sisters."

"Yeah, I'm happy about that."

"So am I," Eve said. And then, suddenly she gripped her belly, and the blood drained from her face. "Oh."

"What's wrong?" Ruby rose halfway out of her seat.

Eve waved her off. "Nothing. Just a bout of queasiness. I get that sometimes. But I'm… I'm okay."

Ruby sat down, relieved.

Seconds ticked by before the color returned to Eve's face. "Pregnancy sometimes knocks you for a loop, you know."

Ruby didn't know. None of her friends had children yet, so she didn't have any firsthand knowledge of the subject. She knew how mares gave birth and had pulled foals on the ranch under the supervision of her father, but the whole human pregnancy thing was new to her. "How do you mean?"

"Well, first off, you get all these weird sensations. In the beginning, you're hungry all the time and feel like you can't get enough food in you. One day, and I'm ashamed to admit this, I consumed two omelets for breakfast and a thick foot-long sandwich for lunch, and I still had room for a barbeque chicken dinner with chocolate cake for dessert. I inhaled food in those early weeks. I couldn't believe it."

"Eating for two?"

"More like an army," Eve said, her eyes twinkling. "But that's passed. Now I'm sensitive all over." She pointed to her chest. "I'm full and tender here all the time."

Ruby froze up, holding her breath tight in her throat. The only thing moving were her eyes. And they were blinking rapidly. She'd been feeling those very sensations lately, too. If she put her bra on too hastily, her nipples would tingle and actually hurt. The pain was foreign to her, and it would take a while before it disappeared. She hadn't thought much of it, but now, as she took another glance at the mountain of ice cream sitting in the refrigerator case, her stomach grumbled. She was still hungry. She could do major damage to those big cartons. Chocolate. Strawberry. Vanilla. And every other flavor.

Good God. Had she missed her period this month?

"Ruby?"

She tried to calculate back in her mind.

"Ruby, you're turning green right before my eyes. Are you okay?"

Ruby stopped blinking and focused on what Eve was saying. She forced herself to recover from the shock and shoved her doubts to the back of her mind. "I'm fine. Um, are you ready to see the best Cool Springs has to offer by way of shopping? It's no Rodeo Drive, but there's a shopping district that has some pretty neat boutiques."

Eve's brows knit together as she subtly scrutinized her, making Ruby wonder if she'd actually fooled her. "Sure, I'd love to. We can walk off the ice cream calories." Eve reached across the table to touch her hand. "Thanks for making me feel welcome in Cool Springs. I think of us as friends already." There was a flicker in Eve's eyes that said she was willing to listen if Ruby needed to talk.

"I feel the same way," she replied genuinely.

Astute as Eve was, Ruby suspected she had already guessed about her involvement with Brooks. But admitting it would make it all too real, and there would be questions she couldn't answer. And feelings she'd have to face. About Trace. About Brooks. And the wrinkle that she might be carrying a child even though she'd been very careful, was all too much for her right now.

It was better to put her head in the sand and let the world keep on turning for a while.

Nine

Brooks gave the living area of his cabin a final once-over. Dozens of roses he'd had flown in from his hometown were arranged in vases and glass bowls all around the room. Their unequalled beauty and sweet scent reminded him of the woman who had stolen his heart. He had pillar candles ready to flicker at the strike of a match. Ideally tonight, after the Christmas party, he would finally show Ruby how much he cared about her.

It had been days since he'd touched her, days since he'd held her in his arms and kissed the daylights out of her. He totally understood that Ruby was torn in two by the return of her ex. She'd banked her future on Trace Evans and had envisioned a life with him. And Trace had failed her. The guy wasn't good enough to shine

Ruby's boots, and tonight was Brooks's chance to win her over. To show her that they needed more time together, that what they'd started at the C'mon Inn was worth pursuing.

In just a few hours, he'd be face-to-face with her, and he wouldn't let up until Ruby was his.

A knock at his door shook him out of his own head. It was his brother Graham.

"Hey."

"Hey. Thanks for showing up on time."

"My brother calls and I come."

Graham stepped inside the cabin, immediately took in the romantic setting, lifted his nose in the air and grinned. "Smells like a funeral home in here."

Oh man, Graham was such a pain sometimes. "Don't make me sorry I let you in here."

"You're doing this for Ruby?" Graham walked farther into the room.

"Yep. You know I don't like to lose. And Ruby is worth winning."

Graham eyed him carefully. "Just don't blow it, Brooks. Seems weird saying this, but she's family now. And you'd have the entire Preston house come down on you if Ruby gets hurt."

"I don't intend to hurt her," Brooks said, hearing the commitment in his voice.

"Man, you're really hooked, aren't you? I mean, you two are polar opposites."

"Let me worry about that. And we're not that different when it comes right down to it."

"Hey, I have my hands full with wedding plans and the baby coming. I'm not going to say another word, except you deserve to be happy." He looked over the place again. "Nice touch with the candles. Ruby will love what you've done. I hope it works out."

The sincerity in Graham's voice made up for his crap from earlier. "I appreciate that."

"So, what's up?"

"I've been thinking."

"About Bill Turner? I do plan to see him one day, but after what you told me, apparently there's no rush. He won't know who I am, right?"

"Probably not, but if you need to see him, to meet with him, I wouldn't stop you. Ruby said…" Brooks paused. Everything Ruby had told him was true. She'd gotten him through a tough day, and that was only one of the reasons he was crazy about her.

"What did Ruby say?" Graham asked.

"A lot, and I'll tell you later, but first I want to run something by you. I think I'm ready."

"Ready?" His brother gestured to the decked-out room. "Obviously, if you've gone to so much trouble for Ruby—"

"I'm talking about my vendetta against Winchester. I think I'm through, Graham. Once and for all. I wanted to get your opinion. I want to make peace."

His brother's brows shot up. "Really?"

"Yeah. It's time. Being here at Look Away has cleared my head some. I'm not the same man I once was. Vengeance can be taken only so far before it destroys you. Coming here made me see that I want to look to the future and not bury myself in the past. What's done is done."

"I like what I'm hearing, Brooks. And Eve will be grateful if you could put the past behind you. She's come here to support me in meeting my father while her own father is very ill. Sutton isn't long for this earth. Eve, Nora and Grace are struggling with all of it. I mean, say what you might about the man, but he is their father, and he's dying."

Brooks drew breath in his lungs. He'd had a long-running feud with Sutton Winchester and had come to learn the man hadn't been guilty of many of the things Brooks had once believed. Winchester's biggest crime had been to love his mother, Cynthia, so much that he hadn't revealed her secrets. In a way, that had been honorable. Though it had caused the Newport sisters a lot of grief, Brooks's anger had softened recently. "Yeah, I know."

"I've already put the past behind me, for Eve's sake and for the sake of our baby. It's no good clinging to a grudge. I'm a happier man for it and I think you would be, too." Graham slapped him on the back. "You've got my full support."

"Wonderful. I'll make that happen soon. Now get

out of here. I've got to get ready to sweep Ruby off her feet tonight."

Shortly after his conversation with his brother, Brooks got dressed in a Western tux, a bolo tie and a black Stetson. He took a final look at himself in the mirror. This was it. He would make his stand for Ruby's affection tonight and, he hoped, make this Christmas holiday one of the best ever for both of them.

Any doubts warring in his head were quickly replaced with positive thoughts as he exited his cabin and approached the Preston home. Surrounding oak, cottonwood and white birch trees glimmered with thousands of lights. The path leading up to the house sparkled from the ground up, and an array of colorful twinkling lights outlined the beautiful home's architecture.

Peace settled in his heart.

A part of him had always known there was something more for him than city life. A part of him had always known something was missing. Now, as he gazed at this home in all its magnificent yet simple splendor, a sense of true belonging nestled deep down in his bones.

Beau greeted him at the door with a big papa bear hug. The man was not ashamed of wearing his emotions on his sleeve, and Brooks hugged him back with the same enthusiasm. "Welcome, son. The party's just getting started." Beau smiled wide, his eyes bright. "My dream of having my whole family under one roof is the best gift I could ever receive."

Brooks got that all too well. Except for Carson, everyone who mattered most to him now was right here at Look Away.

"Let me introduce you and Graham to some of my closest friends."

Brooks followed his father into the house. But as he began shaking many hands and making small talk with Beau's neighbors and friends, he kept one eye on the front door.

And then she walked in.

Ruby.

He swallowed a quick breath. And then excused himself from a conversation that couldn't compete with the stunning creature removing her coat at the front door. She wore her hair partly up in a sweep secured with rhinestones, the rest of her raven tresses flowing down her back. The dress she wore was ruby red, the color perfect for the holidays and perfect on her. The dress exposed her olive skin, dipping into a heart shape in the front that cradled her full breasts.

His heart beat wildly at the vision she made. And suddenly, his legs were moving and his focus was solely on her. He couldn't seem to get to her fast enough as he strode the distance to put him face-to-face with the Ruby of his fantasies.

"Ruby, you look incredible." He hadn't seen her since he'd visited his grandfather. "That dress on you... is a knockout."

"Thank you." She gave him a smile. "You do a pretty good version of a cowboy for a city dude."

"I tried."

"I love the tie on you." She gave it a sharp tug. "And the hat."

He removed it immediately. "Uh, sorry. I, uh…" Why was he tongue-tied?

"It's cool, Brooks." She took the hat from his hand and set it back on his head. "I like the look. Don't take it off on my account."

He ran his hands down his face. Tonight any guests with eyes in their heads would figure out that Brooks had it bad for Ruby, and he wasn't about to hold back. No more pretending. No more hiding out. He was ready to make his claim on her. "Come with me for a second?"

"Sure, but where are we going?"

"You'll see." He took her hand and tugged her through the festively decorated rooms until they reached the kitchen doorway, out of sight to all but a half-dozen caterers. Her knowing eyes glittered. "Look up."

Mistletoe again, and this time she understood exactly where she was and what he was about to do.

He brought his mouth to hers. From the moment their lips met he was a goner, lost in the taste and pleasure and sweetness of her. It was too hot, too amazing to let up. He'd waited for her, craved her and now she was in his arms and he didn't give a good goddamn who saw them or what they thought about it. He was consumed by Ruby. She was his anchor. He'd never had feelings this strong or powerful. The little throaty sounds she was making turned him inside out. She wasn't immune to him. They worked. And he had to make her see that.

"Ruby," he murmured near her ear, the desperation coming through clearly in his voice. "I miss you like hell."

She lifted up on tiptoe and whispered, "If you're talking about making love, I miss you, too."

"Oh, yeah, I am," he said, but he was talking about much more. And he had to bide his time until the end of the evening to show her just how he felt about her. "For starters."

"Starters? Sounds promising, Galahad." Her breath fanned over the side of his face, making his nerves go raw. This woman was a tease, but he didn't mind as long as her teasing was aimed his way. At least she wasn't refusing him. Had she made up her mind about Trace?

"Come back to the cabin with me. We can leave the party right now."

Ruby set a hand on his chest and tilted her head to look into his eyes. "No, we can't. Beau has waited too long to have you here with him."

She had a penchant for being rational and right, and if Brooks wasn't so damn head over heels for her, that would have annoyed the life out of him.

"Just enjoy the party, Brooks."

"As long as you're by my side, I can do that." God, the truth in that was powerful.

"That's where I want to be, too," she whispered.

Brooks breathed a sigh of relief. He had to be respectful of his father and his new family. Wisely, Ruby had put him in his place. He was glad of it, but it was torture just the same.

Christmas music with a country twang streamed into the house, and it seemed everyone was beginning to make their way to the backyard to listen.

"It's a local country band," Ruby offered. "They're pretty good. Beau's hired them for the night."

"Yeah, he told me about them. TLC or something?"

"It stands for Tender Loving Country," she said.

"There's a dance floor set up. Will you dance with me?" He offered her his hand.

"Of course."

And they walked outside hand in hand and danced under the electric warmth of strategically placed heaters. The night was cool, but thankfully devoid of Texas breezes that could make your hair stand on end. Brooks didn't need the artificial heat blasting from the heaters, though; he was already revved up enough inside just holding Ruby in his arms.

"They *are* pretty good," he whispered, nuzzling her hair. She smelled of something tropical and exotic. He brought her as close as he possibly dared. He didn't want to make her uncomfortable—he'd gotten her message loud and clear—so he'd bide his time until he could get her alone in his cabin.

Where he would lay his heart on the line.

They danced every dance until the band took a break, and then Brooks led her off the dance floor. She began fanning herself. "That was fun, but I'm afraid I've got to go...*powder my nose.*"

Brooks chuckled. Ruby was something. He was about to suggest escorting her, but she was snatched away immediately by Eve and Serena. What was it about women going to the john in groups? He'd never understand that.

Toby walked up and caught him red-handed staring at Ruby's shapely ass. "So, you've got the hots for Ruby, huh?"

Brooks gave his half brother a sideways glance, unsure how to answer that.

"It's okay. We get it."

"We?" Brooks turned to face him.

"My brothers and me. We've all had a crush on her at one point or another in our lives, but Dad put a halt to any of that. Let's just say he didn't nip it in the bud—he slashed it to the ground until it was crushed to a pulp. But that was years ago, when we were teens."

Brooks swallowed hard. "That so?"

"Yeah, she's just our little sis now."

"Beau's plenty protective," Brooks said, his voice trailing off as he stated the obvious. He felt an ache in the pit of his stomach.

Toby noticed his change in demeanor and must've taken pity on him. "Actually, when Dad was out here watching the two of you dancing, he was smiling. Maybe he doesn't think it's so bad, you and Ruby. I'd say go for it."

Clay walked up, looking distracted as his gaze scoured the guests milling about. "Have you guys seen Ruby?"

"Who wants to know?" Toby asked.

"Trace Evans is outside the house. He's pretty liquored up, and he's asking to see her."

Brooks blinked. "He's crashing the party?"

Clay shrugged. "I suppose. He wasn't invited."

Now the back of Brooks's hair really did stand on end. He didn't want the guy within fifty feet of Ruby, much less snatching her away from the Christmas party in a drunken state. "I'll take care of it."

Toby gave Clay a crooked smile. "He's a Preston, all right."

It was a compliment Brooks appreciated. "Tell Ruby I'll be back soon." And then he stalked off, ready to face his rival head-on.

Brooks found Trace leaning against his pickup truck, taking a chug from a bottle of whiskey. Wearing jeans and a chambray shirt, his hat tipped back off his forehead, he wasn't exactly dressed for the occasion.

"What do you want, Evans?"

Trace shot back a hard glare. "Ruby. I want Ruby."

Brooks ground his teeth at Trace's possessive tone. "She's not coming out here to see you."

"She'll see me. I have things to say to her."

Brooks held his temper in check. "Now's not the time. She's enjoying the party."

Trace's lips pulled into a twist, and he pointed his index finger straight at Brooks. "You don't speak for her, Newport."

"Why don't you get the hell out of here and sober up. Better yet, I'll get someone to take you home. You're in no shape to drive."

Trace threw his head back in a hearty laugh and gestured with the bottle. The amber liquid inside sloshed back and forth. "What? You mean this? You're obviously not a Texan. This is nothing. Trust me, greenhorn, I'm not blistered. And I need to see Ruby."

"Why, so you can lie to her and hurt her again?"

"You don't know squat about me and Ruby. We had something real special and I made a mistake, is all."

"You made *a lot* of mistakes. Like screwing a married woman. Yeah, I know about your mistakes, Evans. You owe thousands from gambling, and you got kicked off the rodeo circuit for banging the rodeo boss's wife. Now you need Ruby to bail you out."

Evans came toward Brooks with venom in his eyes. "What are you doing snooping into my private life?"

Brooks stood firm. He could take Trace if it came to a fistfight. "Ruby deserves much better. So yeah, I

hired an investigator and found out all your dirty little secrets."

"You son of a bitch. I was going to tell her all about
it. That's why I needed to see her."

"It's too late to confess your sins, Evans. Just give
up."

"I have no plans of doing that. Ruby loves me."

"Yeah, well, she's been loving me lately."

Evans's free hand fisted, and his eyes hardened to
stones. "I should knock you to hell and back."

"I'm shaking in my boots." Brooks shouldn't have
let the guy get to him. He would've never betrayed Ruby's trust like that otherwise. He wasn't a kiss-and-tell
kind of guy. But hearing Evans say Ruby loved him
was like a knife twisting in his gut.

"How much cash would it take for you to leave Ruby
alone?" Brooks asked. "I want you out of her life, *for
good.* Twenty-five thousand? It's enough to cover your
gambling debts. I'll write you a check right now."

"Asshole. You think everything can be settled with
money."

"*Fifty* grand?"

Evans's brows rose in interest. "You bartering for
Ruby?"

"I'm trying to protect her." The man's pride was
keeping him from grabbing the brass ring. Brooks had
to press him. "I'll make it a *hundred* grand. You want
the deal or not?"

A loud gasp came from behind them, and his stomach clenched in dread as he pivoted around. Ruby stood just five feet away, her arms tight around her middle and her eyes spitting red-hot fire. The burn seared through him like a scorching poker. "Ruby, how long have you been out here?"

"Long enough to hear you both acting like jerks."

"Hey, he was the one trying to buy me off," Evans shouted.

"And you were about to accept my offer."

"Don't listen to him, Ruby." Evans took a step toward her.

She put up a halting hand that said, *Don't you dare come close*. Unfortunately, the gesture was meant for Brooks, too. "I. Am. Not. Going. To. Listen. To. This. I'm done with both of you. You can go straight to hell." With that, she spun on her heel and marched away, her shoulders ramrod stiff but the rest of her body trembling.

Brooks watched helplessly as she walked away. Her words cut deep, but nothing hurt as much as seeing the disappointment and accusation on her face.

"Looks like you blew it, Newport."

"Screw you, Evans."

Brooks took off after her, following her to the steps of the house. "Ruby, wait!"

She spun around instantly. The big, fat tears welling in her eyes stopped him in his tracks. "Leave me alone, Brooks."

Serena and Eve stepped out of the house just then

and, noting Ruby's upset state, immediately ushered her into the house, flanking her like a human fortress. With a turn of their heads, the two women shot him glares that could have downed an F-16.

He ran his hands over his face, pulling the skin taut. Then he punched the air out of frustration. He should've known Ruby was enough of her own woman not to need his interference. Had he learned nothing from the past?

Now she was hurt and furious.

It was the last thing he wanted.

And yet somehow, he ended up being the bad guy in all of this.

In black spandex and her comfy Horses Are a Woman's Best Friend sweatshirt, Ruby sat on her sofa, going over the events from last night in her head. Her emotions had been on a high after spending the better part of the evening with Brooks, but when she walked outside and found him in a bidding war *over her* with Trace, she couldn't believe her ears. Brooks had been trying to pay her ex off to stop pursuing her, as if Ruby couldn't make that decision on her own. As if he had the right to decide for her. The worst of it was facing the fact that she really didn't know Brooks Newport at all. Was he the ruthless manipulator that she'd read and heard about? Was he trying to control her? Or had he really believed he was protecting her?

Her phone buzzed and she glanced at the text. It was Brooks again. He'd called and texted her last night until after midnight, apologizing in every way imaginable. She'd refused to answer any of his messages, but in each he'd called himself an imbecile, a jerk or a fool for hurting her, and that had put a smile on her face. The lofty, self-confident man was trying. She had to give him that.

But today's text was different. Today he wrote,

I'm going to Chicago today to make all things right in my life. And then I'm coming back...for you.

A warm shiver ran up and down her body. "Oh, Galahad."

Her doorbell chimed and she rose, checking the peephole before opening the door. Eve had called earlier to check up on her and invited herself over. Ruby was grateful she had. She needed a good friend today, and Eve was quickly becoming that. "Good morning."

Eve's warm smile immediately faded. "Oh, Ruby. You look exhausted. I bet you didn't get a wink of sleep."

"Maybe an hour or two. Come in."

"Are you sure? I can come back later if you want to rest."

"Heavens, no. Moping around isn't my thing. I could use the company."

Eve entered and wrapped her arms around Ruby, pulling her in tight. The hug was exactly what she needed at the moment. "I'm sorry you're upset."

"I'm...yeah. I guess *upset* is the right word. My emotions are all over the place."

"I'm here if you want to talk," Eve said.

Spilling her heart out wasn't easy, but Eve was a thoughtful listener and someone Ruby knew she could trust. They entered the living room and took seats on the sofa next to each other.

Ruby faced Eve and didn't hold back. She told Eve everything about Trace, how she'd fallen for him and waited for him like a fool all those months. She explained how he'd returned to Cool Springs and laid his heart on the line, trying his best to make up with her, offering her everything she'd wanted from him, a life… a future. None of the things Brooks had ever hinted at. She explained about meeting Brooks for the first time at the C'mon Inn and how they'd hit it off from the start. How surprised she'd been the next day to find out that he was one of Beau's long lost sons.

Last night, after dancing with Brooks, she'd finally come to realize she wasn't in love with Trace anymore. And that was before she'd heard about his indiscretions. That was before she'd learned he was trying to use her to bail him out of a financial jam.

"As painful as it is, Ruby, at least you know the truth about Trace Evans," Eve said. "You can cross him off your list. I'm sorry he hurt you, but you dodged a bullet. And don't be mad at me for saying this—Brooks did you a service by exposing him."

Ruby lowered her head and rubbed at her temples. "My brain knows you're right, Eve. But my heart… isn't so sure."

"According to Graham, Brooks is crazy about you. Believe me when I say this. He wouldn't have gone to this extreme with Trace unless he was all in with you. Brooks has his flaws when it comes to confronting adversaries, but he's passionate in what he believes and a really good guy."

"Do good guys take off at the first sign of trouble?" She searched Eve's earnest face, hoping to gain better perspective.

Eve took hold of her hand, and her warmth seeped into all of Ruby's cold places. "He went to Chicago for all the right reasons, Ruby. He's making his peace with the past. Graham and I believe it's so he can come to you with an open heart, as cliché as that sounds."

"No, that sounds…pretty good. If I can believe it. He hasn't stopped messaging me."

"Maybe you can cut the guy some slack?"

Ruby smiled. "Maybe."

Eve took both of her hands now, holding her gently at the wrists, and adjusted her position on the sofa to face her full-on. "I have something for you, Ruby. I hope I haven't overstepped a line here, but…" She released her wrists to dig into her handbag and came up holding a pink rectangular box. "Being in your shoes a few months ago, I kind of recognize the signs," she said, softening her voice.

Ruby's eyes widened. She wasn't ready for this. But maybe it was time to stop procrastinating. It wasn't like Ruby Lopez not to face life head-on. She took the box from Eve and, seeing the concern on her face, gave her a smile. "Do you always walk around with an extra pregnancy test in your purse?"

Eve chuckled. "Oh, Ruby, I was worried how you would take it. You might think us city people are too pushy."

Ruby shook her head. "Yeah, well, city folk are more upfront, I will say that. Country folk tend to gossip behind your back. It all washes out the same."

"It's okay, then?"

"Of course. I should've done this myself. I think I needed the nudge."

"You think you might be?" Eve's voice escalated to a squeak, and a twinkle of hope sparkled in her eyes.

Ruby shrugged. "I don't know. I'm eating like the world is ending tomorrow, and lately I get supertired. Emotionally, I'm a wreck. But that just might be Brooks's doing. I guess… I'll find out soon. Thank you, Eve."

"You're welcome. I'll get going now and let you rest." Eve stood up and Ruby didn't try to stop her, although resting was the last thing on her mind. Her grip on the pregnancy test tightened. She had some major thinking to do, no matter what she found out.

She walked Eve to the front door, and they hugged. "Call me if you need to talk again," Eve whispered.

"I will. And thanks again." Ruby closed the door behind her and leaned against it. Sighing, she glanced at the pink box with light purple lettering in her hand. To think, peeing on a stick could change her life forever. Ruby placed her hand on her belly, and tears misted her eyes as she made a heartfelt wish.

Something she hadn't done since before her daddy passed away.

Ten

Brooks stood on the threshold of Sutton Winchester's master bedroom as one of his nurses laid a plaid wool blanket on his lap and turned his wheelchair around. Brooks came face-to-face with his adversary. With a man he'd hated so powerfully, he'd wanted to destroy him. Now, his emotions raw, he hoped to God that Winchester would hear him out, because he was also the man who had loved his mother dearly and had fathered his younger brother, Carson.

"He's having a good day today, Mr. Newport," the nurse said.

"I'm glad to hear it," Brooks responded as he and Winchester exchanged glances. "Good afternoon, Mr. Winchester."

Cancer seemed to have sucked Winchester's one-time bluster and hard-nosed demeanor right out of his frail body. Hunched over, he appeared a shell of the man Brooks had opposed so vehemently in the past. Warm-colored walls, floral bouquets and December sunshine streaming in the windows contrasted sharply with the sterile environment of medical equipment, drips and tubes, and the constant *blip, blip, blip* of a monitor over the soft music piping in from hidden speakers.

With a feeble wave of his hand at the nurse, Winchester stopped the music. "You know me well enough to call me Sutton, boy."

"Okay, thanks. I will."

"Did you come here to gloat?" He lifted his head to look into Brooks's eyes.

"No, sir, I would never do that."

"Have a seat," the older man ordered in a voice that had long lost its depth.

Brooks sat in a chair three feet from Sutton's wheelchair. "Thank you."

"How is my Eve?" he asked.

"She's doing well. Graham brought her down to Texas, as you know. She's looking wonderful, excited about the baby."

Sutton turned his head to gaze out the window. "That's good. I want my children to be happy."

"Sutton, I know how much you loved my mother."

Slowly Winchester turned his head back and raised his brows, looking him square in the eyes. "Cynthia was a special woman. I wished she would've told me about Carson, though. She left me without telling me she was pregnant. I missed out on my son's life."

"Mom had a lot of pride."

"She was a stubborn one." His eyes twinkled as if he admired that trait. As if he'd loved every single thing about Cynthia Newport. He and Brooks had that in common.

"I'm glad you loved her, Sutton. I'm glad because if you didn't, she wouldn't have had Carson. So I guess I have you to thank for my brother. And I'm doing that now. Thank you."

Sutton stared at him and then acknowledged him with a nod. "I have no intention of cutting Carson out of my will, by the way. As you can see, I'm not long for this earth. Carson is my son and an heir. He will get what is rightfully his."

It had been a bone of contention these past months, something that had grated on Brooks. That his younger brother wouldn't be acknowledged by his father. That he would lose what was due him, being an heir to the Winchester fortune. Carson had already been robbed of a father growing up—they all had—but this was one thing that could make things right in principle. "Carson knows that now. It wasn't ever about the money."

"We have agreed that when the time comes," Sutton said, speaking slowly, "his inheritance will go to charity. That's fine by me. Whatever the boy wants. He deserves it." His voice crumbled a little. "I have many regrets when it comes to Cynthia. Things I should've done differently with her. I lived my life a little recklessly, but I never betrayed her trust. I never told her secret. Seeing how it hurt you and Graham, maybe that wasn't the smartest thing to do."

"We've all made mistakes. I'm here to make peace between our families. I'm here to tell you that I was wrong for pursuing vengeance against you. I was wrong to try to destroy Elite Industries. I understand why you kept my mother's secret all those years. I've only just recently come to understand the crazy things one will do out of love. I, uh, I get it now. So I'm throwing in the towel. I've ordered my attorneys to back off. There'll be no more legal battles. No more disparaging comments to the press. No more trying to undermine you or your company. I've already spoken to Eve, Nora and Grace about this. I've made my peace with them. But I wanted to face you in person. To say it's over."

Sutton nodded, the movement slight, all he could manage. "It's over."

All those months of personal attacks and secrets and truths coming to the surface were finally coming to an end. There would be no more harsh statements, conniving or retribution. The Winchester-Newport feud was done. Finished.

Brooks had one more thing to accomplish to unite the families. "That being said, I'm also here to invite you and your family to Cool Springs for Christmas. On behalf of my father, Beau, and his family. We'd all like the Winchesters to share the holiday with us. Carson and Georgia will be coming. And your daughters are onboard if you think you can make the trip. I'll send a private jet, and you'll have expert nursing care while you are there. I promise you'll be as comfortable as possible. It'll be a time of healing for all of us."

Sutton inhaled slowly, closed his eyes and seemed to give it some good thought. "I'd like to be with my family for Christmas. One last time. Yes, I'll make the trip."

Brooks put out his hand, holding his breath. There'd been a lot of bad blood between them, but he hoped they could put it all behind them. Sutton glanced at Brooks, then slowly offered his frail hand. It was putty soft, devoid of any strength, but he shook with Brooks and then smiled. Something Sutton Winchester rarely did. "It's a deal."

"Deal," Brooks said. "I'll work with your staff to make the arrangements."

"Thank you."

Brooks sighed in relief. He was making strides, and it felt like a heavy weight had been lifted from his shoulders. He was free now to head back to Texas and make things right with one hot gorgeous woman. He only hoped Ruby would agree to see him. She was a stubborn one, too. She hadn't answered any of his messages. Which worried him. But once he returned to Look Away, he vowed not to take no for an answer.

Brooks stood on the veranda with Beau, looking out at the cloudless night. There were hundreds of stars

CHARLENE SANDS   201

decorating the Texas sky, twinkling brighter than he'd
ever seen before. He hugged his wool coat around his
middle against the chilly winds. The Douglas fir tree
decorating the veranda released the fresh scent of ev-
ergreen. It was Christmas Eve, and to spend it with his
father for the first time locked up his fate good and
tight. Brooks knew what he wanted to do with his life.

"Well, Dad. Here I go. Wish me luck."

"You won't need luck, son. Just tell the truth. There's
power in that, and you'd be surprised how much it's
appreciated." Beau faced him. "I certainly appreciated
hearing it from you tonight."

Beau wrapped his arms around him good and tight,
drawing him close. Beau was a hugger, and Brooks
loved that about him. When they broke apart, his father
said, "I'm behind you one hundred percent."

He had his father's love and support and, like a young
boy would, he beamed inside. "Thanks, Dad."

"All right now, go. I've got a houseful of guests I
don't want to neglect."

The Winchesters had arrived this morning, and Beau
had been a cordial host. Any awkwardness that might
have occurred had been wiped clean straightaway by
his father's warm hospitality.

"I'm going. I'm going."

Beau grinned and pivoted around to enter the house,
leaving Brooks alone to make his move. He took a deep
breath and sighed, a smile spreading across his face.
What the hell was he waiting for?

Holding Ruby's image in his mind, he climbed down the steps and walked the distance to her cottage. A light was on in her living room, which was encouraging. He took a moment to gather himself and then knocked. When nothing happened, he knocked again, harder this time. "Ruby, it's Brooks."

Silence.

He reached for his cell phone and called her number. When no one answered, he sent her a text.

Still no reply.

He closed his eyes and sent up a prayer. He hoped he wasn't too late. He hoped Ruby hadn't gone back to Trace Evans. Though he couldn't imagine it, Brooks knew she had a soft spot for the guy. Who knew what lies Evans might have told her to claim his innocence? Had Brooks waited too long? Had his lack of commitment sent Ruby back into Trace's arms?

Brooks's shoulders sagged. He'd stand out here all night waiting for her, but catching pneumonia out in the cold would be a fool thing to do. He had no other option but to go home and try to speak with Ruby tomorrow. She'd be at the house bright and early for Christmas breakfast.

His hopes plummeting, he began the trek to his cabin, wishing now he'd thought to drive. The wind kicked up, lifting his hat from his head. He caught hold of it right before the darn thing sailed away and kept it flattened to his head as he walked on.

Oh man, his bones were chilled, and he had no doubt

it was going to be a long, cold, sleepless night for him. Once he reached his cabin door, a wreath of pine and holly berries greeted him, something that hadn't been there when he'd left for Chicago three days ago. The staff or maybe Beau himself must've put it up as a way of welcoming him back. Or maybe it was simply a Preston tradition to decorate every door on the ranch. Christmas cheer seemed especially important on Look Away.

Brooks entered the cabin, and as soon as his boots hit the wood planks, warmth rose up and smacked him in the face. It went a long way in taking the chill off from his cold trek. The fireplace crackled, and his gaze traveled to the tangerine flames partially lighting the room. He stepped farther inside, removing his coat and hat, rubbing at the back of his neck and wondering about the fire.

"Brooks?" Ruby's soft voice had him turning toward the bedroom doorway.

As soon as he spotted her, his breath caught tight in his throat. She stood at the threshold clad in one of his white dress shirts, the sleeves pushed up and the tail reaching to midthigh on her gorgeous legs. Firelight christened her face and was reflected in her dark chocolate eyes. The lovely vision she made heated his blood, and hope sprang to life inside his body. Good God, she was beautiful.

And *here*.

"I hope it's okay. Beau gave me the key to the cabin."

Tongue-tied, Brooks barely got the words out. "No, uh, it's fine."

"I did some decorating."

He tore his gaze from her to scan the room. A tree sat on a corner table. This one would make Charlie Brown proud. The awkward branches were filled with tiny ornaments and multicolored lights. It was a clear winner and perhaps his favorite Christmas tree ever.

Centered in the middle of the dining room table, a big glass bowl of shiny red and green Christmas balls caught his attention. Atop the mantel, a family of snowmen and Santa trinkets along with cinnamon-scented pillar candles added to the holiday warmth.

"I like it." He was a little dumbfounded, standing there, drinking in the sight of Ruby in his cabin after days and days of no communication. "So, does this mean you're talking to me again?"

"If you want an answer to that, you'll have to come here."

"Baby, you don't have to ask twice." Her subtle, familiar scent, sheet of glossy hair raining down her back and mysteriously sexy voice lured him in. He took the steps necessary to come face-to-face with the woman of his fantasies, giving him the little boost he needed to lay his heart on the line. He'd been a fool not to claim her before this. Not to tell her what she meant to him.

"I like your shirt," he said, tracing a finger on her rosy lips, then skimming it along her sweet chin to her neckline and down to the hollow where the shirt dipped into her mind-numbing cleavage.

"Ask me why I'm here."

"With you dressed like that, I'm supposed to think straight?"

She chuckled, the deep sound coming up from her throat catching him off guard. "Try."

"You picked me?"

"Galahad, it was never really a contest. Trace isn't the man for me."

"You ditched him?"

"I told him I didn't love him anymore. That we weren't meant to be. I'm not happy about you bribing him, but afterward I had a heart-to-heart talk with him, and he was honest with me about everything. He's messed up his life and swore up and down that he never meant to hurt me."

"And you forgave him?" *The cheater, the creep*, Brooks wanted to add, but he was in too hopeful a mood to press his luck.

She nodded. "It's easier when you're no longer emotionally invested. He'll get on the right track again. He got an offer to do a reality show on a country cable television station, and he jumped at the chance. He'll be moving to Nashville soon."

"That's good to hear, because I wouldn't have let you go. I wouldn't have given up on you."

"Because that's what white knights do?"

"Because I'm crazy about you, Ruby. I'm out of my mind in love with you."

Ruby's face brightened, and she smiled. "I love you too, Brooks. This isn't a passing thing for me. This is the real deal."

Thank God.

He didn't need the mistletoe above their heads for permission to kiss her. He circled his arms around her waist and brought her up against him. Her chin tilted, and he gazed into the most stunning pair of dark eyes he'd ever seen. The glow in them promised more than he could ever hope for. Ruby was going to be his. And then his mouth came down on hers, meeting her flesh to flesh. Her soft lips slid over him exquisitely. Her petite body, all five-foot-two of her, crushed against him and put his brain in jeopardy of shutting completely down.

He broke the kiss to her defiant whimper and then dipped down to lift her. Her brows arched in question, but she didn't stir otherwise. Her arms automatically roped around his neck, and he carried her to a chair beside the sizzling fire. A log broke apart, and golden flames climbed the height of the fireplace, bringing intense heat. He sat down in the warmth, and Ruby wiggled in his lap. But Brooks had to contain his lust for just a few more seconds. "Ruby, I thought I'd blown it with you. Foolishly I left town without telling you how I felt about you. Maybe I shouldn't have had Trace investigated..."

"You think?"

"Okay, I get it. It wasn't my business to interfere, but I was trying my best to protect you from getting hurt again. Ever since the night we met at the C'mon Inn, when that guy was pestering you, I've had this need to protect you."

"Are you apologizing?"

"For not trusting in you? Yes. You're more than capable of making up your own mind about things."

She gently took his hand in hers and stroked his fingers, sending tingles up and down his arm. "I didn't mind the first time, Brooks. I thought it was really kinda sweet of you, coming to my rescue. You didn't know me, and still you were willing to help me. But with Trace, it was different. I really don't want to talk about him anymore tonight. It's over and done with. I know in my heart you had good intentions."

"I did and I still do, sweetheart. Actually, you call me Galahad, but in truth, you're the rescuer in this duo. You've saved me, Ruby. From the very moment I met you, my life changed. I've become a better person, a more tolerant man, because of you. I came here looking for my true father and found a new way of life, as well. I've discovered something within me that I wouldn't have realized if not for you. You taught me about the ranch and how things work in the country, but you also helped ease the pain of my past. Coming with me to meet my grandfather for the first time meant a lot. That was a hard reunion, but having you there comforting me and showing me how to let go worked miracles for me. You helped me turn away from the past and look forward. To the future. You gave me something special that day. You made me see what my life could be."

He lifted her fingertips and kissed each one. Just looking at her filled his heart with so much joy, he could hardly think straight. "I've always felt something was missing in my life. I thought it was because of my childhood. I thought it was because I never knew my father. In a sense, that's true. I missed knowing Beau as a boy, having his guidance and love, but I've come to realize I've also missed this place. Look Away and Texas. It feels right being here, with you. I've known only city life, but now that I'm here, I don't want to leave. I'm going to work it out so that I can stay closer to my family. The company is in good hands. I can run it long-distance."

"You're staying?" The hope in Ruby's voice swelled his heart.

"I want to, yes. I hear there are some pretty nice ranches for sale close by." Brooks rose with Ruby still in his arms. Her warmth mingled with his, and as soon as he lowered her down and her feet touched the floor, he felt the loss. "I went to your place looking for you. And nearly died when I couldn't find you."

"I had a surprise for you, Brooks."

"Having you here was the best surprise I could ever hope for," he said. And then he dropped to one knee and gazed into a pair of astonished eyes as firelight caressed her beautiful face. "Ruby Lopez, I promise to love and cherish and yeah, probably protect you for the rest of my life. I can't help it. I'll always be your Galahad." He fished inside his pocket for the wedding ring he'd brought with him from Chicago, a diamond ring that had once been his Grandma Gerty's. It was all he had left of the woman who'd taken his family in during a precarious time in their lives.

Brooks held up the ring, and it glistened under the firelight. Clearing his throat, he presented it to her and said, "Ruby, this ring was given to me by my grandmother. She told me one day I'd give it to a special woman. That day has come, sweetheart. I want to give you this ring and along with it, my heart and soul. I ask that you do me the honor of marrying me. Ruby, will you be my wife?"

Tears spilled from Ruby's eyes, raining down her face without warning. Brooks held his breath, hoping they were happy tears. "I went to Beau and asked for his blessing, Ruby. I asked him for your hand in marriage, and he was touched and happy for us."

"Oh, Brooks," she said, grasping his wrists as he rose. "That's the sweetest thing…"

Facing her now, he stared into her eyes, waiting patiently for her answer. "Ruby?"

She began nodding quickly, the tears still trekking down her cheeks. "Yes, Brooks. I'll marry you. I'll be your wife."

He laughed, and the sound of his relief and joy filled the room. "You had me worried there, sweetheart."

"No, no. It's just that I didn't expect this."

Using the pads of his thumbs, he wiped at her tears, carefully drying her eyes. Cupping her face, he said softly, "I didn't expect it, either. It happened so darn fast, but it's the right thing. For both of us. I promise you, Ruby, we'll have a great life."

"I know we will." And then she took his hand and walked him over to the scraggly Christmas tree. Turning to face him, she smiled sweetly. "You've given me this beautiful ring and a promise of your love. It's a wonderful gift, and now I have a gift for you, my sweet love." She handed him a small box decorated with snowmen and reindeer wrapping paper. "Merry Christmas."

He lifted the lightweight box in his hands and jiggled it. Nothing moved. He shot her a glance. She gave nothing away, and he had no idea what she was up to, but her expression was hopeful, and her eyes positively beamed. "Let's see," he said, ripping away the wrapping and opening the small box. After separating the tissue paper, he lifted out a small white garment.

"It's called a onesie," Ruby said softly.

Puzzled, Brooks read the printed saying on the front. "Future Look Away Ranch Wrangler."

He blinked. And blinked again. Normally he wasn't slow on the uptake, but this...this was like a lightning bolt striking his heart. Something else lay at the bottom of the box. Cute, small, adorable tan leather baby boots.

He stared at them for a second. "A *baby*? Ruby,"

he said, tears burning the backs of his eyes so hard he could barely get the words out, "are we having a baby?"

She began nodding her head. "Yes. We're going to have a baby, Brooks."

Joy burst inside him, and his face stretched wide as he grinned. Thankfully he didn't shed tears, but his emotions were off the charts. "A baby…" he said, awed, as he pulled Ruby back into his arms and kissed her cheek, her chin and finally her lips. "It's the best Christmas gift in the world."

"Yes," she whispered. "I think so, too. But I wasn't sure how you'd feel…"

"I love you, Ruby." He set his hand very gently on her belly. "And I love our baby already. I couldn't be happier. To have you and our child in my life, it's a dream come true."

"I love you, too. You'll be a great father, Brooks." Ruby covered his hand with hers and positioned it where new life was growing inside her. Then she leaned in to kiss him. The kiss bonded them together forever, and Brooks had never been happier in his life. He was complete. His life held new meaning and purpose.

Here on Look Away Ranch, he had finally found home.

Epilogue

Christmas morning on Look Away was usually a chaotic affair of eating, joking, opening gifts and spreading the love, and today was no different, except that the family had expanded to include the Winchesters. Ruby had coordinated with the household staff to make sure they were as comfortable as possible.

Sutton Winchester had his own set of nurses, and the older man who'd played a role in Brooks's, Graham's and particularly Carson's lives was holding his own this morning. His wheelchair was right next to the warm flames of the fireplace, and he seemed to be in good spirits. Occasionally Ruby would see him smile at his daughters, Nora, Grace and Eve. For a powerful man who wasn't long for this earth, his eyes still held a bit of mischief, and though he spoke seldom, what did come out of his mouth was witty and charming.

Ruby knew the history he had with Brooks's mother. Last night, while in bed with her new fiancé and father of her unborn child, Brooks had recounted to her all he'd known of their relationship. Sutton was Carson's father, and it was sad that Carson had come to know him only in the last months of his life.

"Gather around the tree, everyone," Beau said after they'd eaten a Christmas morning meal that would probably stay with them throughout the entire day. Except for her. She was still ravenous. And now Brooks was watching her like a hawk, eyeing her with love in his eyes, but also concern over every little move she made. It was sweet, for now, as they were both getting used to the idea of her pregnancy and overjoyed at the little one who'd be making an appearance in eight months.

Married now, Nora and Reid Chamberlain took their places along with newly engaged Grace and Roman Slater. Carson stood with his fiancée, Georgia, next to Sutton's wheelchair, and his allegiance to his ailing father was inspiring. Toby, Malcolm and Clay were to Beau's right, and next to him on the other side were Graham and Eve.

Brooks grabbed Ruby's hand and angled them beside Graham.

"Want to sit down?" he asked her.

"No, I'm fine," she told him quietly. Ruby's heart was thumping wildly in her chest. No one knew their news yet, and she was enjoying this special secretive time with her new fiancé, but a part of her just wanted to scream it from the rooftops. The ring, which she'd hated taking off, was in Brooks's pocket.

Lupe came around with a tray of mimosas and sparkling cider. Brooks snapped up two ciders and handed Ruby one, giving her a quick, adorable smile.

"Thank you all for making the trip to Look Away for the holiday," Beau began, holding up his glass. "I'm not one for making speeches, but it seems lately there's a need. So I'll make this toast short. The past has been hard on many of us. But looking around this room, I have renewed faith in the future. I see love here in many forms, and it's heartwarming."

Beau's gaze found hers, and his smile made Ruby blush down to her toes.

"I, for one, am grateful that Graham and Brooks are here with me this holiday. They have met their three half brothers and our Ruby, and it's been all that I had hoped. And I'm so happy having Carson here, along with all you wonderful Winchester girls and your father. It's all a blessing.

"I cannot hold a grudge about the past. It serves no purpose and so, with that in mind, I hope that this coming together of the Prestons, Newports and Winchesters brings with it peace to all families. Let's set aside our differences, put salve on our wounds and try to move forward. Especially at this time of year, when goodwill abounds, let's have ourselves a very Merry

Christmas." Glasses clinked and good-natured chatter began. The families were united and, at least for this holiday, all was well.

"Dad, if you don't mind, I'd like to say something." Brooks's tone was reverent, and everyone stopped talking to listen.

"Of course, son."

Brooks's arm came around Ruby's shoulder, tugging her in even closer, and many sets of eyes rounded in surprise. "I didn't know what to expect when I came to Look Away. I'd been hell-bent on finding my father, as everyone here knows. And when I finally met him… well, when I met you, Beau…" Brooks said, speaking directly to his father now and choking up a bit. Ruby put her arm around his waist, supporting him. She'd always be there for him when he needed her. "When I met you, Beau, saw you for the decent, kind man you are, I was floored, inspired and thrilled to know you. To be your son. But I also felt one with this land. It was like a part of me became suddenly alive again. And I knew I belonged here. I knew that Texas and Look Away was my real home. Ruby played a role in that."

He spoke to her now, and she lifted her chin to look into his eyes. "Ruby and I have fallen deeply in love. With Beau's blessing, I've asked her to marry me, and she said yes. We are officially engaged as of last night." Brooks dug into his pocket and formally put the ring on her finger.

Applause and congratulations broke out. Brooks bent

his head and brought his lips to hers, giving her a taste of the passion that would always consume their lives. She had no doubt.

"There's one more thing," Ruby said, raising her voice above the din. Everyone grew silent again. "It seems that Graham and Eve aren't the only ones who will be making Beau a grandfather."

Gasps broke out, and Ruby thought she heard Eve chant, "All right!"

"Brooks and I are going to have a baby."

Tears poured down Ruby's cheeks again. Even though she tried her best to maintain decorum, she couldn't help it, and Brooks did his best to wipe them away.

Beau was the first to come over, wrapping his arms around both of them and hugging tight. "Congratulations, you two. I couldn't be happier." His voice broke, and Ruby knew he was crying, too. "You've got yourself a wonderful girl, son."

"I couldn't agree more," Brooks said, brushing a kiss across her cheek.

After everyone congratulated them and the Christmas festivities moved on, Brooks took her by the hand and led her outside to the front veranda. Wrapping his arms around her from behind, he bestowed kisses on the back of her neck as they swayed back and forth in full harmony, gazing out on the land, the pasture, the horses, all that was Look Away. "We're going shopping tomorrow," he announced quietly.

"For baby things?"

He chuckled. "First I need to put a roof over our heads, sweetheart. We're buying our own ranch, one we can call home. And even though I'm in real estate—"

"You're not *in* real estate. You're the king of real estate."

"But you're the expert in ranching. I value your opinion in all things, but I especially defer to you when it comes to Texas and ranches."

"You're letting me choose?"

"I want you to have your heart's desire, Ruby. The house, the ranch. I'll build it for you if you can't find something you absolutely love."

"I already have."

Brooks's brows arched. "You found a place?"

"I found something I absolutely love."

And then she roped her arms around his neck and kissed her handsome fiancé something fierce with all the love she had in her heart, thanking her lucky stars she'd met her very own knight in shining armor that night at the C'mon Inn.

"You, Galahad. I found you."

* * * * *

COMING NEXT MONTH FROM

Available January 3, 2017

#2491 THE TYCOON'S SECRET CHILD
Texas Cattleman's Club: Blackmail • by Maureen Child
When CEO Wesley Jackson's Twitter account is hacked, it's to reveal
that he has a secret daughter! Amidst scandal, he tracks down his old
fling, but can he convince her he's truly ready to be a father—and a
husband?

#2492 ONE BABY, TWO SECRETS
Billionaires and Babies • by Barbara Dunlop
Wallflower Kate Dunhem goes undercover as a wild child to save her
infant niece, but a torrid affair with a stranger who has his own secrets
may turn her world upside down...

#2493 THE RANCHER'S NANNY BARGAIN
Callahan's Clan • by Sara Orwig
Millionaire Cade Callahan needs a nanny for his baby girl, but hiring his
best friend's gorgeous, untouchable sister might have been a mistake!
Especially once he can no longer deny the heat between them...

#2494 AN HEIR FOR THE TEXAN
Texas Extreme • by Kristi Gold
Years after a family feud ended their romance, wealthy rancher Austin
reunites with his ex. Their chemistry is still just as explosive! But what
will he do when he learns she's been withholding a serious secret?

#2495 SINGLE MOM, BILLIONAIRE BOSS
Billionaire Brothers Club • by Sheri WhiteFeather
Single mother Meagan Quinn has paid a price for her past mistakes,
but when her sexy billionaire boss gives her a second chance, is she
walking into a trap...or into a new life—with him?

#2496 THE BEST MAN'S BABY
by Karen Booth
She's the maid of honor. Her ex is the best man. Their friend's wedding
must go off without a hitch—no fighting, no scandals, no hooking up!
But after just one night, she's pregnant and the baby *might* be his...

HDCNM1216

*When CEO Wesley Jackson's Twitter account is hacked,
it's to reveal that he has a secret daughter! Amid
scandal, he tracks down his old fling, but can he convince
her he's truly ready to be a father—and a husband?*

Read on for a sneak peek at
THE TYCOON'S SECRET CHILD
by USA TODAY *bestselling author Maureen Child,
the first story in the new*
TEXAS CATTLEMAN'S CLUB: BLACKMAIL *series!*

"Look where your dallying has gotten you," the email
read.

"What the hell?" There was an attachment, and even
though Wes had a bad feeling about all of this, he opened
it. The photograph popped onto his computer screen.

Staring down at the screen, his gaze locked on the
image of the little girl staring back at him. "What the—"

She looked just like him.

Panic and fury tangled up inside him and tightened
into a knot that made him feel like he was choking.

A daughter? He had a child. Judging by the picture,
she looked to be four or five years old, so unless it was
an old photo, there was only one woman who could be
the girl's mother. And just like that, the woman was back,
front and center in his mind.

How the hell had this happened? Stupid. He knew how
it had happened. What he didn't know was why he hadn't

been told. Wes rubbed one hand along the back of his neck. Still staring at the smiling girl on the screen, he opened a new window and went to Twitter.

Somebody had hacked his account. His new account name was, as promised in the email, Deadbeatdad. If he didn't get this stopped fast, it would go viral and might start interfering with his business.

Instantly, Wes made some calls and turned the mess over to his IT guys to figure out. Meanwhile, he was too late to stop #Deadbeatdad from spreading. The Twitterverse was already moving on it. Now he had a child to find and a reputation to repair. Snatching up the phone, he stabbed the button for his assistant's desk. "Robin," he snapped. "Get Mike from PR in here now."

He didn't even wait to hear her response, just slammed the phone down and went back to his computer. He brought up the image of the little girl—his daughter— again and stared at her. What was her name? Where did she live?

Then thoughts of the woman who had to be the girl's mother settled into his brain. Isabelle Gray. She'd disappeared from his life years ago—apparently with his child.

Jaw tight, eyes narrowed, Wes promised himself he was going to get to the bottom of all of this.

Don't miss
THE TYCOON'S SECRET CHILD
by USA TODAY *bestselling author Maureen Child,*
available now wherever
Harlequin® Desire books and ebooks are sold.

www.Harlequin.com

Whatever You're Into… Passionate Reads

Looking for more passionate reads from Harlequin®?
Fear not! Harlequin® Presents, Harlequin® Desire and
Harlequin® Blaze offer you irresistible romance stories
featuring powerful heroes.

◆ HARLEQUIN *Presents.*

Do you want alpha males, decadent glamour and jet-set
lifestyles? Step into the sensational, sophisticated world of
Harlequin® Presents, where sinfully tempting heroes ignite a
fierce and wickedly irresistible passion!

◆ HARLEQUIN *Desire*

Harlequin® Desire novels are powerful, passionate and
provocative contemporary romances set against a backdrop of
wealth, privilege and sweeping family saga. Alpha heroes with
a soft side meet strong-willed but vulnerable heroines amid a
dramatic world of divided loyalties, high-stakes conflict and
intense emotion.

◆ HARLEQUIN *Blaze*

Harlequin® Blaze stories sizzle with strong heroines and
irresistible heroes playing the game of modern love and lust.
They're fun, sexy and always steamy.

Be sure to check out our full selection of books
within each series every month!

HPASSION2016